GORILLAZ IN THE TRENCHES 2

Lock Down Publications and Ca$h
Presents
Gorillaz in the Trenches 2
A Novel by *SAYNOMORE*

Lock Down Publications
Po Box 944
Stockbridge, Ga 30281

Visit our website @
www.lockdownpublications.com

Lock Down Publications
Like our page on Facebook: Lock Down Publications @
www.facebook.com/lockdownpublications.ldp
Book interior design by: **Shawn Walker**
Edited by: **Mia Rucker**

Stay Connected with Us!

Text **LOCKDOWN** to 22828 to stay up-to-date with new releases,
sneak peaks, contests and more…
Thank you.

Submission Guideline.

Submit the first three chapters of your completed manuscript to ldpsubmissions@gmail.com, subject line: Your book's title. The manuscript must be in a .doc file and sent as an attachment. Document should be in Times New Roman, double spaced and in size 12 font. Also, provide your synopsis and full contact information. If sending multiple submissions, they must each be in a separate email.

Have a story but no way to send it electronically? You can still submit to LDP/Ca$h Presents. Send in the first three chapters, written or typed, of your completed manuscript to:

LDP: Submissions Dept
Po Box 944
Stockbridge, Ga 30281

DO NOT send original manuscript. Must be a duplicate.

Provide your synopsis and a cover letter containing your full contact information.

Thanks for considering LDP and Ca$h Presents.

Acknowledgements

First, I would like to thank God and my Lord and Savior Jesus Christ for all the blessings in my life and all the hard times for walking me through them.

Much respect and love goes out to the Lockdown Publication family for believing in me. Big shoutout goes to Ca$h. hands down, respect and love Bruh!

Love and respect goes to all my family members Baby Sha and Nene. Daddy loves you, hands down. Always remember that. Never forget that. Amityville, NY. 11701 Stand up baby. Albany Ave and Smith Street we here. Pillz , Tuggy, Sha-p, Fat-tee, LA, Mo, Willie, Dererick, Munchie, Kavin dapp, TT pretty J.Rock, Davon, A-Dog, Tory, SNL, Alana, Loud. I just got one word to say. Browns.

Law 19

Know who you're dealing with— do not offend the wrong person.

SAYNOMORE

Prologue

A-Dog sat quietly as he waited for his name to be called. It's been five years since he's seen the street. The last thing he remembered was the car flipping over and waking up in the hospital one year later. It ain't take the judge two weeks to sentence him to two to five years in prison. He remembered the day he walked in, and today he waits for them to call his name so he can walk out. Adem Smith A.K.A. A-Dog, walked to the front desk in I.D., got his property, and two officers walked him out the prison's front gates.

"A-Dog! What the fuck? My nigga home." Pillz walked up to A-Dog and gave him a pound and a hug.

"It's good to be home and out that bitch. I'll be in a body bag before I go back in there."

"Man, you out now. Where you tryin' to go first?"

"Take me to go see Murder, bro."

Pillz looked at A-Dog and nodded.

A-Dog stepped out of Pillz's car and walked to Murder's headstone. "Damn, man. Shit fucked up how things played out with you. It feels like we was just together yesterday. I broke down when word got back to me you was killed in a prison riot. I should have been there with you but I'm sure the streets remember your name. I love you, bro." A-Dog kissed his fingers and touched Murder's headstone before getting back in the car with Pillz. "Who got the streets on lock now?"

"Nobody. Niggas playing the block again. Ain't nobody got no work like that after you and Murder's wave. The block been dead."

"Well, it's time to give the block a heartbeat again. I'm home."

"I'm glad you are. So where you staying at now?"

"My peoples set me up a spot on Cosated Drive, so you can just drop me off there."

"Cool. I'm glad you are home, A-Dog."

"Thanks, bro."

Pillz pulled up in front of A-Dog's apartment and let him out. He watched as he walked inside before he drove off.

A-Dog looked around the one-bedroom apartment. There were two bags on the bed. He opened them and saw two pairs of Timberland boots, socks, T-shirts, boxers, two sweat suits and a black 9-millimeter pistol. A-Dog got dressed and walked out the door.

He walked to Miller Avenue and looked at the house Murder called home. He walked around the back of the house and looked in the window. The house was abandoned. He picked the lock to the back door and went inside. He looked around before going upstairs to the master bedroom. Murder had a trick door put in the closet. A-Dog opened it and walked inside. He saw two duffle bags with eleven kilos of cocaine, $290,000, and Murder's .45 pistol lying next to the bags. A-Dog picked up bags and walked out the door.

Chapter One

A-Dog pulled up at Pillz's house. When he stepped out the car, he looked around the house. In five years, nothing had changed.

Pillz opened the front door and looked at A-Dog as he smoked his blunt standing in the front door. "It's been a few days. I thought you forgot about me."

"Hell to the no. I just had a few things lined up; shit to put in order. The question is: You ready to get shit poppin'?"

"Hell yeah. I'm ready to bleed the block with that A-one shit you got."

"Good, come on. Let's get this understood with us."

Both men walked in the house. Pillz passed the blunt to A-Dog as he closed and locked the door. A-Dog looked at Pillz and nodded as he pulled the bricks of cocaine out his book bag and placed them on the kitchen table.

"Yo, that's that same shit we used to have?"

"Yeah, I had a nice stash put up before me and Murder got knocked."

"So, we dealing with the same prices?"

"Naw, I'm pushing for forty on each one of these. I got to make up for loses and I need every dollar to know what the new plug is talking about."

"I respect that."

"That's love, my nigga. I respect how you respect the game. How long before you knock it off?"

"Give me thirty days on this so I can work my ones and twos."

"Copy that. Here's my number. Hit me when you ready to see me, in about thirty."

"Say less."

SAYNOMORE

Chapter Two

A-Dog quietly sat in the parking lot in his black Range Rover as he waited for Mo'nay to come eat at the Village Diner, something she did twice a week. He hadn't seen Mo'nay in five years and he needed to talk with her. This was his third day at the diner waiting for her. He was hoping today would be the day she pulled up. He checked his phone for the time and looked at her G-wagon pull up. He watched as she stepped out of the truck and walked into the diner. He stepped out of his truck and followed her inside.

Mo'nay looked up at A-Dog as he walked to her table and took a seat. "A-Dog, when did you get out?"

"About two weeks ago."

"I'm glad to see that you are home. Get up and give me a hug."

A-Dog smiled as he got up and gave Mo'nay a hug.

"I'm sorry to hear about Murder."

"Yeah, that shit was fucked up. They got my nigga down bad. So how you been, Mo'nay?"

"Good, staying out the way, but I know you ain't come to my favorite food spot to ask me how I was doing. So, you going to tell me why you really here?"

"I need a plug with good prices like before; someone I can trust."

"I may have a plug, but after what happened with Omar and Pete, they hide their faces behind a mask and only go through a middleman. You cool with that?"

"I guess I'll have to be. Find out the prices for me and let me know. Put my number in your phone." After giving Mo'nay his number, they talked for a few more minutes before A-Dog left the diner.

SAYNOMORE

Chapter Three

It's been three weeks since A-Dog talked to Mo'nay. He hadn't heard from her since, but he wasn't rushing to hear from her. He still had ten kilos he'd cut down and stretched into sixteen. Plus, Pillz was still working on the one kilo he had given him already. He was driving down Sun Raise Highway when he noticed that Omar's old detail shop door was open. He walked inside.

"Hey, can I help you?"

"No, I was just looking around. I thought this shop was closed down. I didn't know they had reopened it. I used to come here to see Omar and Pete."

"You knew Omar and Pete?"

"Yeah, I did."

"Hold on, wait here for a second. I'll be right back."

A-Dog watched as the man walked off to the back of the shop. A few seconds later he motioned for A-Dog to follow. A-Dog walked through the back doors to the same office he had five years ago and saw a heavyset man seated in Omar's chair. In front of the desk was a tall, skinny man, standing like Pete used to.

"Please, come in and have a seat. My guy told me you knew Omar and Pete."

A-Dog looked around before taking his seat. "I did. I knew both of them."

"Let me introduce myself. I'm Manny and my friend's name is Jake. And you are?"

"My name is A-Dog."

"Well, A-Dog, tell me how you knew Omar."

"I used to do business with him. Me and my homie Murder— may he rest in peace."

"You friend is dead?"

"Yeah, five years ago. When we both went to prison he got killed."

"I'm sorry to hear that. So, tell me, what type of business you were doing with Omar?" A-Dog looked around before saying a word. "You can talk in here, A-Dog. Trust me."

"He used to supply us. The last shipment we picked up was twenty car tires; thirty for each one."

"That was the last pickup?"

"Yeah, we got locked up not even two weeks later."

"So, what happened to the twenty kilos?"

"We got off ten of them before we got locked up."

Manny opened the desk drawer and pulled out a green book. He opened the book and turned it around for A-Dog to see. It had the date, time and day of the last pick-up Murder received in it and the balance they still owed. "One thing I know about business is that it always comes back in a circle, A-Dog. Omar told me about you and Murder and how Murder would do all the talking. He said you were hungry and how you took over blocks like water filling up cracks when it rains. So, I'm thinking you came by here today because you are looking for a new plug so you can pick back up where you left off."

"Yeah, I was hoping for that in a sense."

Manny leaned on the desk in front of him. "A-Dog, I see truth in your eyes when we talk. I can open up that door for you again but there's only one problem stopping me."

"And what's that?"

Manny pointed at the balance A-Dog and Murder owed in the green book. "Half a million dollars is a lot of money, A-Dog. How can we do business with old business not taken care of yet?"

"Give me ten weeks and I'll be back with your money. After that, can we continue where we left off at?"

"Sure, we can, at thirty a piece, A-Dog."

A-Dog wrote his number down on a piece of paper and handed it to Manny. Manny did the same thing.

"So how are you going to come up with this money in ten weeks with no work?"

"When we got locked up, they only got a quarter of a tire off us, and like I told you when we first started talking, I got ten of them already I'm working with now."

"Okay, A-Dog, I will see you in ten weeks."

A-Dog got up and shook Manny's hand and walked out of the shop, back to his truck.

"Manny, you trust him?"

"Everything he said was truthful. He looked directly in my eyes when he talked to me. He wasn't trying to hide nothing."

"You don't think he had nothing to do with Omar and Pete's murders, and the three hundred kilos of cocaine that was stolen from us?"

"A man with three hundred kilos of cocaine wouldn't have come by here to hope to meet someone who can still supply him. He had nothing to do with it. He probably don't even know the drugs were stolen, to be honest, but only time will tell."

**

"Yo, Pillz, I see you got the block rocking again with that A-one pure shit."

"Already K-P. What? you tryin' to pick-up?"

"Just a little twenty-eight from you."

"Cool, that's going to run you one point five."

"Shit, let's do it, fam."

"Let me go get the scale real quick. I'll be right out."

"So, we ain't going dry no time soon?"

"Hell to the naw."

"Copy that."

Pillz counted the money up then passed K-P the work. He watched as he left the trap. Pillz rolled a blunt and was thinking about the twenty grand and a half a kilo left. The way shit was going, he would be sold out in the next few days or so. The block was his now, and he was going to let it be known.

**

"Damn, girl, that feel good as hell. A nigga missed how you get down, beautiful." A-Dog had his eyes closed as Tasha was sucking his manhood in the driveway of her house off of Albany Avenue in A-Dog's Range Rover.

"I missed you too, daddy. You going to cum for me?"

"Hell yeah, don't stop. Keep going just like that, baby girl." A-Dog closed his eyes and held Tasha's head as he released all his juices into her mouth. Tasha swallowed it all as she looked up at him and smiled.

"Damn, you going to make a nigga fall in love with you, shorty."

"Whatever, A-Dog, you got all the game." Tasha smiled as she reached into the ashtray, picked up the blunt and relit it. A-Dog was looking out the window when he saw Tuggy walk up to Kent across the street in front of the *Friendly Barbershop*.

**

"Yo, Kent, what's up with that baby love. It's been too long, my nigga."

Kent looked at Tuggy as he smoked his cigarette. "I told you I got you, but right now the bread that I got is to take care of some other stuff I got going on right now. You just got to wait until I take care of this other business first."

"What the fuck do that got to do with me? I got my own shit I'm dealing with right now and I need that check today. Fuck what you talking about."

"Look, Tuggy, that shit over with. You act like you want to hit. We can get our cleats dirty if that's what you trying to do. As far as that money, that shit is over with, on God."

"On God, my nigga? You tough like that?"

"You just got to swallow that shit until next time."

Tuggy licked his lips and smiled as he pulled out his .38 Bull-dog. "Naw nigga, swallow this, on God!"

Kent fell backwards as bullets ripped through his chest. Tuggy stood over Kent and shot him three more times as he lay on the ground before he took off running. Kent's body was soaked in blood as he lay with his unseeing eyes open, dead to the world.

**

"Oh shit, Tasha, look I got to get the fuck up out of here before the police come. I ain't trying to deal with no part of this shit."

"Damn, who just bodied Kent like that."

"I don't know or give a fuck who did it. I'm telling you I got to go. Hit my line later tonight."

"Okay, I will."

"Tasha, go in the house. You ain't seen shit."

"I know, I know." Tasha got out of the truck and walked in the house.

A-Dog pulled off as people started coming out of their homes to see what happened. He made a left on Sun Rise Highway. He couldn't believe what he had just seen. He knew he needed a killer like that on his team for the shit he had planned. One who took no shit and Tuggy had just passed the test.

SAYNOMORE

Chapter Four

"Head crack, pay me my fucking money and I'm taking the bank. It's a hundred a pop. Let me see how many of you niggas is balling now." Pillz was talking shit as he counted his money and smoked his blunt.

"Yo, Pillz, you heard that Kent got clapped yesterday? Laid out in front of Friendly Barbershop?"

"What the fuck? By who?"

"Shit, the block ain't talking. They laid him out at like two P.M. I was told."

"Damn, I just seen that nigga like two weeks ago too." Pillz phone went off. "Yo, hold up, Mo, I got to take this call. A-Dog, what's good fam?" He answered.

"Where you at? We need to link up. I need to talk with you. Plus, I want you to take a ride with me."

"I'm over here in P-Town. You about to pull up?"

"Yeah, I'll be there in twenty minutes, homie."

"Copy that. I'll be out front when you pull in."

"Cool."

"Yo, Mo, look, I got to go take care of some shit. I'm rolling out. Ya nigga can have the bank. I'll get that free money from you next time." Pillz dapped Mo up as he walked off the front of the apartments to wait on A-Dog. A few minutes later he saw A-Dog pull up in a black Range Rover. "What's up A-Dog, what's the word?"

"Shit, look, I need somebody in these streets I can trust. Me and Murder was two of the same kind, thick as thieves. I need to know that I can trust you like that because when shit get hot, we need to be blazing. I need to know you can do more than sell dope out of a house." A-Dog looked at Pillz as he was driving down one ten.

"Hell yeah, if a nigga try us, off with his head. I'm down for the one eight seven. I got your back, my nigga, hands down."

"That's what the fuck I'm talking about. Let's get paid. Now I got to find this nigga, Tuggy. You know where he be at?"

"That nigga be at the Pinks from what I'm told."

"Shit, let's go check it out." When they pulled up to the Pinks, Tuggy was out front smoking a cigarette and talking on the phone. "Yo, I'll be right back. Let me go holla at son real quick."

"Do you, fam, I'm right here."

A-Dog stepped out of the truck and walked up to Tuggy. "What's good, fam? Can I get a word with you?"

"Yo, let me call you right back." Tuggy hung up his phone and put it in his pocket. "What's good, homie?"

"Shit, peep game, if you ain't busy, come take this ride with me."

Tuggy looked to see who was in the truck. "Shit, come on, let's ride out. I ain't got shit going on right now."

"That's what the fuck I'm talking about."

Once in the truck, A-Dog lit a blunt and pulled off. "This the move. You know how Me and Murder had shit on lock. I'm out the joint and I'm moving like I was never locked up and I need a nigga like you on the team. Pillz got Overland and Bayview on lock. I'm on Albany Avenue and Smith Street and I need you on Great Neck Road and Miller Avenue. The way I got this shit planned, we all going to eat."

"What's the numbers you talking?"

"Forty a kilo. I need mines off top but you going to make a hundred plus."

"Hell yeah, I'm with that move. You know a nigga like me love the paper."

"Let's get this butter then, baby." A-Dog looked at his phone and saw Mo'nay was calling him, "Yo, y'all hold on. I have to take this call. Yo, Mo'nay, what's good?"

"Nothing, you busy?"

"Naw, what's up?"

"Meet me at Peterson Park."

"I'll be there in twenty minutes."

"I will be here waiting on you."

"I'm on my way now." A-Dog hung up the phone. "Look, Tuggy, I'ma drop you off with Pillz at his spot. I need to go meet someone. Pillz is going to fill you in, and I'll link up with y'all niggas in like an hour."

"Cool."

A-Dog dropped them off and when they were inside, he went to meet Mo'nay.

**

"So, this is how you living, Pillz."

"I'm having my cake and eating it too."

"I see, I see. Let me see what that work look like."

"Cool, check this out while I go get da work. Roll up a blunt while I get everything together. The buds and wraps are over there on the table."

"Word, say less."

Tuggy walked to the table and rolled a blunt while he waited for Pillz to come back.

"Yo, check this out. This is a quarter brick of that pure." Pillz passed the work to Tuggy as he took the blunt from Tuggy and started smoking.

"Damn, you cut this already?"

"Yeah, that's that pure. I'm giving them what they pay for. That's how we lock the block down."

"I respect that. So when is A-Dog going to give me that pack?"

"Shit, he might have it with him when he comes back."

"I don't ask no questions. Just know his word is law at all times."

"Yo, copy that."

**

A-Dog pulled up at the park to see Mo'nay feeding the ducks. He stepped out his truck and walked up to Mo'nay, "I see you have a love for ducks."

"I can't lie, I do. I had two when I was younger. I named them Daffy and Donald."

"That's cute."

"So, I made a few phone calls for you, and I can get you set up with work for thirty-two grand a pop. How's that sound to you?"

"That sounds good, but Omar's people Manny pulled up on me over the last business deal we had with Omar before he was killed. We still owe half a mill in debt to them. So, I'm trying to get that up first."

"So, Manny is up here now?" I should have known he would be taking Omar's spot. Let me tell you now, A-Dog. Manny is not like Omar so watch your step with him. I'm just letting you know."

"What you mean by that, Mo'nay?"

"Just keep your eyes open is all I'm saying. So, after you clear this debt up with Manny, should I expect a call from you?"

"Yeah, I'll try to get ten of them off your peoples."

"Well, you have my number. Call me when you are ready, and I'll put them on standby. And A-Dog, don't be like Don-killer and put all the work into the streets and end up with nothing."

"What you mean?"

"I'm saying. Open up a business and not no barbershop or pool hall. Think different, like an auto part's store or a tow trucking company. So, you can have a record of where your money is coming from. I'm just saying."

"I'll look into that."

"You should. Call me when you ready to see me. I'll be on standby."

"Give me about a week or so." Mo'nay nodded as she walked off.

Once back in the truck, A-Dog's phone went off. He looked and saw it was Mac calling him. "Yo, Mac. What it do?"

"You know I'm living but right now, I'm trying to come see you."

"Word, word, what we looking for?"

"I'm trying to put two of them in a cage."

"You know them Tweety birds are forty a piece."

"Yeah, I be knowing already."

"Shit, let me know when you are in the Ville."

"I'll be at the spot in forty-five minutes."

"I'm waiting on you."

"I'll see you in a few." A-Dog hung up the phone and made his way back to Pillz' spot.

SAYNOMORE

Chapter Five

"What's up, beautiful, I ain't seen you in a minute."

Mo'nay turned around to see one of Ra's homies, Mase, walking up to her. "Mase, oh my God! It's been a minute, how you been?"

"Good, you looking too lovely right now. What you been up to?"

"Just trying to stay out the way. I'm sorry about what happened to your peoples."

"Yeah, that shit still hurt. You know they never found out who killed Rock or Ra but on gang, when I find out, I'ma lay they ass down with no questions asked."

"Trust me, I know how you feel. Ra was my boy. So, what you been up to out here?"

"Just trying to get this money, that's all."

"Ain't we all? Well, take my number and let me know when you trying to reup. I might be able to help you with a deal or something."

"Word, good looking, Mo'nay. I'll call you this week."

"I'll be waiting to hear from you."

"Cool."

Mo'nay got in her truck and thought about how she could use Mase. Just in case A-Dog ain't come through on his part. She ain't knock Don-Killer off and Ra and set Murder up for the fall. She ain't take a gamble with her life against Omar, Killer and Pete just so another nigga could take over Amityville. She would have A-Dog in a bag first before she let him stop her from getting her cake and eating it too. A-Dog was going to work for her whether he knew it or not and if shit got real, Mase was going to get a tip on who killed Rock. Her loyalty was to herself and her money. She didn't mind killing three birds with one stone again.

**

A-Dog pulled up at the detail shop and Jake waved for him to pull the car into the garage.

"A-Dog, it's good to see you again. So, I take it you have everything for me?"

"That's why I'm here."

A-Dog walked up to Manny and shook his hand. He walked back to the car and pulled out the bookbag he'd placed the money inside of, handed it to Manny and followed Manny to his office. He placed the bag on his desk and took a seat. "Half a mill on the head."

"Jake, could you go count that up please?" Jake took the bag and walked out of the office. "I like a man who is honest and who keeps his word. You think you could move another twenty kilos?"

"Yeah, I can. We still dealing with the same price. Thirty a pop?"

"Hold on, let me check." Manny pulled out a book from his desk drawer and saw Omar was selling them kilos for thirty grand a piece.

"Sure, we can still do thirty if you get twenty kilos every time you shop with me."

"And it's the same product. Ninety-seven percent pure?"

"Always, nothing less."

Jake walked back into the office and gave Manny a thumbs up.

"It looks like everything is good on your end. Now, let me take care of my end." Manny nodded at Jake. "So, what's the time frame we are looking at A-Dog?"

"Ninety days, maybe sooner."

"That works for me. Let's go see Jake."

As they walked out of the door, Jake was placing two duffle bags in the back of A-Dog's truck. "I'll see you in ninety days, A-Dog."

"Yeah, you will." Manny patted A-Dog on the back with a smile and returned to his office with Jake in tow.

**

Pillz was at the spot when A-Dog pulled up. He opened the front door to let him know the door was unlocked. A-Dog walked into the house and gave Pillz a pound.

"We good, fam?"

"Hell yeah, I got five with me right now and I put the rest up."
A-Dog put two kilos on the table. "Check that shit out, baby boy."

Pillz pulled out his knife, cut a line down the middle of the brick and sniffed a little bit to see what it was hitting like. "Yo, A-Dog that's that motherfucker right there, hands down."

"I be knowing already, skrap. Yo, give this bird to Tuggy. Let him know it's forty on the head."

"Copy that, I'll handle that business."

"Cool, I got two more drop-offs to make. I'll catch up with you later."

"Say less, fam."

SAYNOMORE

Chapter Six

A-Dog pulled out his phone as he sat in his Range Rover and called Mo'nay. She picked up after the second ring.

"Hello."

"Hey, what's up, Mo'nay?"

"Nothing, just chilling. What's good with you?"

"Same thing. I was calling to let you know that I took my truck to the auto part shop and they gave me a tune up for thirty dollars. My truck is running A one. I was giving you a heads up that I'm staying with my same auto part shop for now. If anything changes, I'll give you a call."

"So, when is your next tune up?"

"He told me he wants to see how my truck is running after ninety days. So, I'll bring it in for another checkup then, but I'm also about to go on one ten to check out the car garage for sale today like you told me to."

"Okay. Keep me posted and call me if you need me. You have my number."

"I will and good looking out, Mo'nay."

"Always A-Dog."

A-Dog hung up the phone and drove off listening to Yo Gotti's Down in the DM.

**

Mo'nay was thinking about the conversation she just had with A-Dog when her phone went off. She looked to see it was Mase calling her.

"Hello?"

"Hey, beautiful, what's up."

"What's good with you, Mase?"

"I was calling to see if we can meet up today. I might need a favor from you, if it's cool."

"Sure, what time you want to link up?"

"How about two at the pool hall?"

"Sure, I'll be there."

"Okay. I'll see you then."

Mo'nay hung up the phone. She knew what she had to do. Mase was going to be her toy soulja to help her secure the crown in Amityville. A-Dog didn't know it yet, but his pack of wild dogs were about to run up against a hungry wolf. Mo'nay went upstairs to put her plan together. The game was about to begin.

**

"Tuggy, I see you out here holding the block down and getting money."

"Naw, my nigga, it just look like that. You can't believe everything you see, homie."

"Tuggy, you too much for T.V. Look, I'm just trying to grab a little twenty-eight grams from you."

"Say less. That's going to run you a light fifteen hundred."

"I got that, fam."

"Well, let's do business then. Kando get da B-love ready, and I'll be right back with that work for you." Tuggy walked to the back room and pulled out an ounce of dope and walked back to the front room. "Ninety-seven percent pure, baby boy. What you know about that? That shit better than pussy."

"Count that up, fam." Kando handed Tuggy the money.

Tuggy sat at the table and started to count. "I like the way you do business. Fifteen hundred on the head. Hit my jack when you ready for a reup and let niggas know I got that snow white on deck."

"It's already out there. The block knows y'all got that snow fall. I'm out, though. I'll catch up with you later."

"Cool, peace, my nigga." Tuggy dapped Kando up as he walked out of the door.

**

Mase watched as Mo'nay pulled up in her white G-Wagon. Mo'nay stepped out wearing a black Chanel top that showed off her stomach with a pair of black and white checkered shorts that showed off her thighs, ass and long legs. Her socks matched her shorts and all white three inch Chanel stiletto's boots. She had on a diamond encrusted bracelet with a complement of similarly dazzling chains and earrings that glistened from within the depths of curly jet black hair that hung to the middle of her back. She sassily swung an Alexander Wang purse as she sashayed into the Sportstown Bar and Grill, commanding the attention of every eye in the room.

Mase got up and met her at the door with a hug. "Damn, you really are a show stopper. All eyes on you today."

"I try to do what I do."

"There's no trying when you step out. Come on, let's go over here and talk out of the range of other ears." Mase noticed everyone watching as she stepped through the pool hall looking like a boss bitch. He purred, "Have a seat, beautiful." once they reached their table. She shot him an amused look as she sat down. "So here's the thing. I'm not going to cut any corners. I could lock this whole side down from Sun Rise Highway to one ten and I got a pack of niggas who going to eat with me. I just need some help getting off my feet."

"Real talk, I respect your gangster, Mase. I always have, but you know the rules of the streets. A favor for a favor. If I wash your hands, you gotta wash mine later. Nothing is free."

"You already know I was raised and birthed in the streets. I know how the game go.

Mo'nay looked into Mase's eyes as he talked. "How long do you think it will take you to move a kilo?"

"Being real, about three weeks. I'm jumping out there fresh again, but I'll play the block all night to move it.

Each kilo is forty-thousand dollars on the front. With money in hand, it's thirty-four thousand. You think you can handle that?"

"Yeah, I can do that with no pressure."

"Good, because I called in a favor from a friend." Mo'nay reached into her Alexander Wang purse and pulled out a kilo wrapped in red tape and handed it to Mase while no one was looking. Mase placed it on the inside of his coat. "Damn, I ain't know you had this on you."

"Bad girls move in silence boo-boo."

"Word, I respect that, hands down."

"Good, I got to run now. I'll see you in three weeks with forty grand I hope."

"Ain't no hope about it. It will be there, my word."

Mo'nay got up, bent down and kissed Mase on the cheek. Then, took her thumb and rubbed away her lipstick print. She walked out of the pool hall with a strong runway strut, knowing everyone was watching her. She got into her G-Wagon and pulled off.

Chapter Seven

Mase walked into the room and looked at LA and Shawn with a smile on his face. He reached inside his coat and pulled out the kilo of cocaine and placed it on the living room table. "We on, niggas."

"What the fuck? Shorty came through. I saw her pull up yesterday but I ain't know she had it like that."

"Nigga, she fucked me up when she pulled it out."

"What's the ticket on it?"

"Forty Gs on the front and thirty-four on delivery. Look let's cook this shit up and get the ball rolling. I got three weeks to get her bread. LA you got the Forties, Shawn you got the back streets to the new homes, and I got the sticks. We pulling all-nighters. We back on and it's grind time. We all got to make thirteen grand a piece. Shorty gave us a blessing, let's not fuck it up."

"Nigga, I'm already making calls."

"That's what I'm talking about, Shawn. Let's get this money."

**

Lil' B walked into the yard where Shay Dog was talking with two of their homies. Lil' B pulled up and said, "Yo, Shay, guess what the fuck this bitch, Tasha just told me not even ten minutes ago?"

"What the fuck she said that got you pulling up in here thirty-eight hot?"

"She said she saw that nigga, Tuggy lay KP down. She was in her front yard when he rocked him to sleep. They was arguing when Tuggy pulled out on him and started shooting. Then, he ran through the cut."

"Wait, you telling me this bitch saw Tuggy body KP?"

"On gang, she just said that."

Shay-Dog looked at Dolow and Dink, then back at Lil' B. "Dead ass. Now that I think about it, I remember KP telling me him and Tuggy was having paper problems with each other."

"Yo, let's ride out on the bitch ass nigga right now."

"Chill, Lil-B. We gonna pull up on him later tonight. It's too early right now. I've been seeing that nigga over by Miller Avenue."

"We need to go eat on that nigga now."

"Yo, I said we chill till later tonight, Lil' B."

"Man, what the fuck?" Lil' B walked out of the yard and up Forty-Fifth Street, refusing to have to hear what Shay-Dog was saying.

"Yo, Dolow, go with that nigga and make sure he don't do no dumb shit."

"Okay, I got you, bro."

Dolow ran up to Lil' B. "Yo, Lil'B. Chill for a minute, homie."

"Naw man, I don't know what this nigga Shay-Dog is talking about. This nigga killed one of our own not even a month ago. I'm going to handle this shit right now. Fuck what he talking about."

"Fuck it then, bro. Let's go take care of the business then. I'm with you." #

"Bet. Let's go pull up on that basehead RC and rent his car out so our shit ain't hot. Plus, niggas won't know it's us."

"Come on then, let's handle the business then."

**

Pillz, I'm going to see the homie, Tuggy to see how shit is looking over there. You straight over here right now?"

"Oh yeah, we smooth, hands down. A-Dog, tell son I said what's up."

"Cool, I got you. I'll be back in like an hour, fam."

"Already."

A-Dog pulled out his phone and called Tuggy. After two rings, he picked up. "Yo, yo what's good?"

"Shit, I'm headed your way now."

"Bet. I'm about to make this play."

"I'll see you in a minute then, fam."

"You know where I'm at."

A-Dog got into his truck and pulled off.

**

"There go that bitch ass nigga right now, walking out the park, Lil' B."

"Yeah, I see him. You ready?"

"Hands down, let's do this."

Lil' B pulled his gun out and drove up to the front of the park as Tuggy was walking out. Tuggy didn't see them in the black Honda as he was putting his phone up.

"Yo, Tuggy, KP said what's up! Tuggy looked up and saw the black Honda as he was putting his phone up. A .45 pistol was pointing out the window at him. All that was heard was the sound of the blast going off. Tuggy pulled his gun and started shooting back as he ran and ducked behind a car.

Lil' B and Dolow were shooting at him, "Yeah, you bitch ass nigga. You ain't think that shit was going to come to light."

"Nigga, fuck you and that dead ass, bitch ass nigga!"

Dolow was standing outside of the car door as he was shooting at Tuggy behind the car.

Tuggy ducked down, trying to decide which way to run. He pulled out his clip and saw he only had three rounds left. "Fuck, fuck, how the hell I let these niggas catch me down bad?"

A-Dog was coming down Great Neck Road, when he saw a black car in the middle of the street, shooting at someone. Then, he realized it was Tuggy. He hit the gas and stopped right next to the black car. When Dolow looked, it was too late. A-Dog was already letting off shots to his chest. His body fell back into the car. Lil' B got shot in the shoulder as he pulled off. Tuggy looked from behind the car and saw A-Dog's truck. He ran and jumped inside. Lil' B lost control of the Honda and hit a street light pole. He looked over at Dolow's dead body in the passenger seat.

A-Dog pulled up to the car as Tuggy jumped out. He pointed his gun at Lil' B's head. "Now, bitch ass nigga, you tell KP I said what's up." Tuggy let off all three rounds into Lil' B's face. He looked at his body, then jumped back into A-Dog's truck and they pulled off. "What the fuck, Tuggy? Who was that?"

"One of KP's people. That nigga Lil' B that be on Albany Ave."

"Them niggas just had you down bad."

"Yeah, he started shooting and talking about tell KP he said, *Hi' and shit.*"

"I don't know how the fuck he found out I bodied son."

"I think I do. We will deal with that later. Right now, we got to dump this truck off before we get pulled over in it."

"You know. That was Shay- Dog's people."

"Fuck that guy."

A-Dog pulled up to an abandoned house, parked the truck in its garage, closed the door and pulled his phone out to call Pillz. "Yo, come get me. I'm on Madison Ave by Fun Zone."

"You good?"

"Hell no. Shit just went sideways."

"I'm on my way right now."

A-Dog looked at Tuggy as he waited for Pillz to come get them.

**

Shay-Dog looked at his phone as it went off. He saw it was Dink calling him. "Yo."

"Bro, you need to get to Great Neck Road, like now."

"What the fuck is going on?"

"The police got everything taped off. Lil' B and Dolow came up here on the bullshit and got themselves bodied."

"Don't tell me that shit, Dink."

"In real life, they dead, homie. I'm looking at this shit right now."

"I'm on my way down there now, Dink."

"I'm in front of the park."

"Copy that."

Shay-Dog hung up the phone, shaking his head as he walked to his car to get to Great Neck Road to see what the hell went down.

Chapter Eight

"Tuggy, what the fuck happened out there?" Pillz was smoking a blunt as A-Dog looked out the window.

"I had a little play to make and took care of some business. Afterwards, I'm coming out of the park and the next thing I know, I'm getting dumped at. So, I start blasting back right before A-Dog pulled up."

"That's three bodies in sixty days, like what the fuck." A-Dog paced the floor as he smoked a C-I, looking at Pillz and Tuggy. "Look, I only remember one motherfucker out there when you laid K-P down and that was Tasha. I had the bird in the truck getting the power mouth at the time and I know for a fact she was fucking that nigga Lil' B. I bet she told that nigga it was you. That's why they came at you like that."

"I'll kill that bitch. That's on Browns."

"Tuggy, you hot right now. We can't afford that shit right now. You can't get caught slipping. Pillz, I need that one eight seven. Tasha's running her mouth and we don't need the wrong ears getting hold of her story."

"I'm on that shit. I'll peter roll that bitch tonight."

"Tuggy, stay ducked off and have the plays come to the house. We need you out of the eyes of the streets right now. Pillz get that shit done tonight, before there's a call to the snitch hotline."

"Copy that."

**

Dink flipped the table over and he walked the floor with his gun in his hand, "What the fuck we gonna do about these Albany Ave, Smith Street niggas? These motherfuckers building a graveyard off our team. We need to show these niggas their shirts ain't bulletproof and they can be laying up in a church facing the ceiling."

"Chill the fuck out, Dink. If we go hit them right now, they going to be on point. They waiting to see what we do and the only nigga we know of right now for sure, for sure is Tuggy. You know where that nigga is at right now?"

"Shit, I can hit the streets and find out. You know the streets be talking."

"That's the point. I'm trying to make sure the streets keep our name out of them. Give it a few days and we will pull out the banana clips. We going to stomp the ground."

"Cool, I'm about to go hit the block and see what I can find out, fam."

"Let me know something A.S.A.P."

Shay-Dog watched as Dink walked out the house. He hoped he could keep his cool out there.

**

Mase was at the bar drinking a beer watching the news when LA walked in and sat next to him. "LA, you seeing this?"

"I was out there yesterday when the news teams was there. It was ugly."

"What they say happened?"

"It was a shootout with them Albany Avenue cats and them niggas just caught the bad end of the stick."

"Damn, but how is that bread coming along?"

"I'm already up ten and I have the whole thirteen grand from the plays in Deer Park, Bay Shore, Crime Dance and Riverhead."

"I be knowing he be on his shit. Hit him up and let him know to be at the spot tomorrow night so we can put this money together to keep this ball rolling."

"I'm about to do that right now and I'll see you tomorrow at the spot, fam."

Mase nodded at LA as he got up and walked off from the bar. Mase took a sip of his beer and continued to watch the newscast.

**

"So, you telling me you saw the whole thing, girl?"

"Yes, I was sitting in A-Dog's truck when he pulled up on KP and started shooting him." There was a knock at the door.

"Tasha, that would have blown my mind if I'd seen some shit like that. I think someone is at your door."

Tasha walked to the door and opened it. "Hey, what's up Pillz?"

"What's good, Tasha. What you got going on?"

"Shit, in here with Lala just smoking and talking shit."

"Yeah, shit I got that gas pack. What's up?"

"Come on in and blaze that shit up. Lala, we got company girl, and he got that gas."

"Lala, what's good, ma? Long time no see."

"I been around. You just been ducked off getting to the money."

"Naw, I'm just living a little. Here, roll this up, ma." Pillz gave Lala the blunt to break down as he pulled a large sack of light green gas out of his coat pocket and placed it on the table.

"Tasha, I've got to ask you something."

"What's up, Pillz?"

"Who you been talking to about KP's Murder. That shit is all in the streets causing me and mine problems."

Lala looked at Tasha when he said that and suddenly stopped rolling the blunt. "I ain't said nothing to no one. It's none of my business." Pillz looked at her and got madder as the seconds passed. He jumped and pulled his gun out, pointing it directly between Tasha's eyes. "You lying bitch! A-Dog told you to keep your mouth shut. Now look at you, starring down the barrel of my gun."

"Pillz, please don't do this, please don't." Lala looked at Pillz and saw the shadow of death in his eyes. She knew he was about to kill Tasha.

"That please shit don't move me bitch. You almost got my nigga rocked." Tasha saw sparks fly from the barrel of Pillz gun and felt a burning pressure force her backwards as several bullets tore through her chest. She fell on the floor and Pillz moved to stand over her, starring down at her glassy eyes with a twisted sneer on his face as he rapidly pumped his trigger finger and launched four more bullets into her chest. He turned to Lala. "Pillz, we go back to the sandbox."

"I know we do. That's why this shit is going to hurt me."

"No!" Lala threw her hands up in front of her.

"I'm sorry, baby girl." Pillz shot her two times in the face, then picked up the sack of weed and the blunt before he walked to the backdoor. He called A-Dog up a few minutes later as he walked through the cut.

A-Dog picked up instantly. "Yo."

"I just rolled two different kinds of gas up in the same blunt and smoked them together."

"So, it's done?"

"I'm in the clouds."

"Say no more then." A-Dog hung up and Pillz stopped to light the blunt Lala had rolled as he walked into the night.

Chapter Nine

"So, what you think?"

"I like it. What's the asking price every month?"

"Two grand."

A-Dog looked around the empty parking lot of the detail shop and nodded, knowing he was making the right choice. "Would you do rent to own?"

"Yeah, we can talk about that if you're interested in owning the place."

"Cool. I like it." A-Dog reached into his pocket and pulled out six thousand dollars in crisp hundred dollar bills. "Mr. Larry, here's two grand for the security deposit and another four to cover the first two months. If it's cool with you, I'd like to fill out that lease now."

Larry looked at the money, then back at A-Dog and smiled, "I like the way you do business. Come on, let's go to the office and get the paperwork done."

"I'm right behind you, lead the way."

**

Mo'nay sat at the bar drinking a Long Island Iced Tea while she waited for Mase to pull up. He wasn't supposed to meet her until three P.M. She was just around the way and decided to get to the bar early and wait. There were not a lot of people inside, only ten or so watching a Jets and Bills game on T.V. Mo'nay cut her eyes at the door and saw Mase, and his two boys walk in.

"Yo, let me handle this business with shorty and I'll join you two in a minute." Mase dapped his boys up and made his way over to Mo'nay. "Let me find out you a Jets fan."

"No boo-boo. I'm a Giants fan all the way."

"How long you been waiting for?"

"About thirty minutes. Can we go talk somewhere?"

"Yeah, let's grab one of the tables in the back." Mase watched as Mo'nay got up and led the way. He couldn't stop starring at her ass until she finally sat down.

"How is business going?'

"Real good. I have that forty Gs for you now."

"That's all you have for me?"

"Yeah, the block is hot right now since a nigga got bodied on Albany Ave. Then, two niggas got it on Great Neck Road after that; and to top that off, two bitches were found dead in a house on Albany."

"Yeah, I saw that shit on the news. You still got some work right?"

"Yeah, like a half a bird."

"So, when you think I should be hearing from you again?"

"Within the next two or three weeks."

Mo"nay looked into Mase's eyes and knew he wanted her to front him another kilo. He just didn't know how to ask her.

"Where the money at?"

Mase looked at her and handed her a fanny pack. Mo'nay opened it up and looked at all the hundreds, fifties and twenties inside. She closed it back and placed it inside of her Gucci bag. "I like the way you came through on your word, Mase."

Mase looked at Mo'nay and greedily licked his lips. Mo'nay looked around the bar before reaching into her bag and pulling out a kilo of cocaine. She handed it to Mase. "That's the last one I can front you. Same time frame, same price. Got it?"

"Yeah, I got you. Good looking, Mo'nay."

"I'll see you in a month, Mase." Mo'nay got up and walked from the back table, out of the bar and to her G-Wagon, never looking back at Mase. She knew the block was hot and that A-Dog and his people also had work. If he was going to sell on the block, she wanted a piece of his pie too.

**

"It's lit up in here tonight and the DJ is fucking with the game." Pillz, Tuggy and A-Dog walked through the club's crowded dance floor to their V.I.P. seats upstairs. They had bottles of Cîroc and Moet on ice waiting for them already. The club lights were dark blue with flashes of white lights going off in time with the tempo of the music. "Don't nobody touch my bottle. This Ace of Spades is hitting." He popped the bottle open and poured it up.

"A-Dog, I'm on that Cîroc tonight with that gas in the air pump."

"Just know, I'm not carrying anybody out of here tonight, Pillz. You and your bottle of Cîroc better be ready to walk out of here tonight."

They all laughed as they popped their bottles. The DJ piped the club up when he started playing Chris Brown's song Lurkin, featuring Tory Lanez. There were women singing along to the song and the DJ was giving shoutouts on the floor piping the crowd up even more.

"Yo, A-Dog, ain't that Red Rum coming up here?"

"Yeah, yeah, that's him. He good, Tuggy."

"A-Dog, what's good, fam?"

"Shit, just trying to have a good time tonight, Rum. What's good with you?" A-Dog got up, dapped Rum up and poured him a drink.

"A-Dog, can I vibe with you for a minute?"

"Come over here and have a seat. What's good?"

"To get to the point, I'm trying to eat with you. You know I got my own little spot to trap out of."

"Word, you know I be knowing. Take my number down and hit my jack tomorrow and we can link up and talk business."

"Yo, that's love, A-Dog. Say less, I'll play your line tomorrow fam, respect.

"Respect, Rum." A-Dog looked past Rum and saw Tuggy tonguing down a bitch who was sitting on his lap. Pillz was standing off to the side smoking a blunt and simultaneously taking a bottle of Cîroc to the face as he talked to some niggas his team was eating with. Everyone was enjoying the fruits of their labor like niggas who owned the block and motherfuckers respected that.

"Yo, Shay-Dog, let me get at you real quick, bro."

Shay-Dog stopped dancing with a dark skinned beauty with a huge ass and walked over to Dink. "What's up, fam? I gotta get back to this hot ass over there before it starts to cool off."

"That nigga Tuggy up there in the V.I.P. popping bottles and shit, like he ain't got a care in the world, and like shit sweet out here. He with A-Dog and that nigga, Pillz."

Shay-Dog looked up at the V.I.P. and saw Tuggy piped up and living the life. "Yo Dink, get ready. We about to light this bitch up for real." Shay-Dog looked at Dink and pulled his gun, a black Glock nineteen, from under his shirt. "Let's do this shit."

"That's what the fuck I'm talking about, big bro."

A-Dog got up off the couch with a bottle of Ace of Spades and a smile on his face, dancing to the music with a tall light skinned woman dressed in a black catsuit and silver heels. He looked down at the dance floor below and spotted Shay-Dog at the end of the crowd, pointing a gun at him. Before he could say a word, bullets were flying through the air, shattering bottles, blowing out lights and sending clubbers scattering for cover. A-Dog got shot in the shoulder, dropping his bottle of Ace of Spades and tumbling over the cocktail table.

"Oh, shit." Pillz pulled his pistol and stayed low as he started shooting down at the dance floor. Tuggy pushed his companion off his lap, pulled his own gun out and joined Pillz, taking shots at both Shay-Dog and Dink. "You niggas want beef? The forty Dogs got plenty bitch! Hope you niggas brought ya appetite!"

Shay-Dog let loose a spray of bullets and ducked behind a table.

"A-Dog, you good?"

"I'm alive. That pussy boy shot me!"

"Them niggas dead, on gang!"

"Yo, we got to get the fuck out of here."

People were yelling and ducking down, trying to avoid getting shot and make it out the door. Tuggy grabbed A-Dog while Pillz covered them, shooting at Shay-Dog and Dink as they made their way to an exit downstairs. "A-Dog, you still with us?"

"Yeah, that shit went in and out. Let's get the fuck out of here before the police come."

Once they made it to the parking lot, they loaded A-Dog in the Range Rover and sped away from the chaotic scene unfolding in the club parking lot.

"Them niggas are already dead. They just don't know it yet. It's just a matter of time."

Pillz silently nodded in agreement as he drove and A-Dog held his shoulder in pain.

SAYNOMORE

Chapter Ten

"A-Dog, you good?"

"I'm a hundred percent, Pillz. I saw that pussy ass nigga pointing the gun at me and I thought I was tripping at first."

"So, what's the move now?"

"Them niggas are going to be on point and waiting for us to hit them back, Tuggy. We just got to chill for right now. Matter of fact, let me make a phone call. I know how to deal with this shit. I'll let them bum ass niggas know they ain't in our league. We gotta stay on point because the money don't stop."

"That's facts."

"Yo, I'm headed to my trap, A-Dog."

"Cool, I'll link up with you a little later, Pillz."

"Copy that."

Tuggy dapped A-Dog up and walked out of the spot. A-Dog picked up the phone and dialed up a friend.

**

"L.A. , how we looking over there?"

"Beautiful, my guy. I already cooked up half this kilo and bagged some up for him. I'm just waiting on him to come pick up, Mase."

Mase walked to the kitchen table where LA was bagging up the cocaine as he smoked a blunt of gas. He watched him weighing everything up. "You heard about the shootout last night at Cloud Nine with them Forty Dog niggas, A-Dog and his crew?"

"Yeah, I forgot who was telling me about that shit last night. They said A-Dog got shot in the V.I.P."

"Yeah, word on the streets is that shit went down because Shay-Dog caught them slipping and decided to pop it off on them. Word is he's the one who shot A-Dog last night."

"It's about time they do something. What, three of they homies got peter rolled by them niggas? They needed to straighten their face up, real talk.

"Yeah, but on another note. What's really good with you and Mo'nay? Shorty tough."

"We just on some business shit. Nothing more. Shorty is about her paper."

"R.I.P. to Don-Killer. He had him a real one. If I was you I'd be doing a lot more than business with her. I would be trying to crack that egg. Big facts."

"Whatever, LA. Just try and finish bagging this shit up. We got money to make. I'm trying to get this forty grand up, plus thirty-four more Gs within the next month, baby boy."

"You know what I've been thinking about, Mase? Letting Shay-Dog in with us. That would be more niggas on the block pushing for us. We already in with the Forties anyway.

"Yeah, that crossed my mind but them boys hot right now. Plus, they got too much shit going on and I don't want their problems to become our problems."

"I feel you on that."

"Look, I'm about to roll out. Let me get that work you got for Shawn, and I'll drop it off to him while I'm out."

"Shit's right there, Mase. What time you pulling back up?"

"Probably like six, maybe seven. I got some shit I need to take care of today."

"Cool, just hit me up when you on your way back then."

"Copy that, say less." Mase picked up the package for Shawn and dapped LA up before walking out the front door.
        **

Shay-Dog walked into the house and dapped Dink up and gave the rest of the homies a pound. "Dink, that's how the fuck you do shit. Catch a nigga sleeping and put that hot steel in they life. Bang bang motherfucker, we don't waste shells because we hit out targets."

"What the fuck you on, man? That nigga looked like he did a backflip over that table when he got hit. You popped his ass!"

"That's because I had one nigga in my sights and wasn't no slugs going to be wasted."

"So, we going to hit these niggas again or what? I ain't trying to wait for them niggas to strike back."

"We're going to chill and see what they talking about first. Now that they know what time it is."

Dink passed Shay-Dog the blunt as he took a seat at the table with the other homies to play dominoes. "Yo Shay-Dog, real talk, you know that nigga A-Dog is going to come back at you. I think we should just keep the heat on them for right now, fam."

"Naw, that nigga ain't stupid. He ain't pulling up in the Forties, so we good for right now. Trust me, Dink, I'll let you know when it's time to hit them up again. But this time, we going to make sure we finish it." Shay-dog was smoking the blunt and thinking about what Dink just said. He was right. The question was what would be A-Dog's next move?

**

"Pillz, I heard about what happened last night in Club Cloud Nine."

"Yeah, that's some crazy shit that went down but that's over and done with. What you trying to grab."

"I need half a bird for the twenty."

"Shit, more like the twenty-five, my guy."

"Damn, it's tax season already?"

"Naw, but I can't give it to you for a lower price than what I pay for it. That would be hustling backwards, J-Jumbs."

"Say less, I got twenty-five Gs, fam."

"Cool, let's take care of business then."

Pillz walked into the house, sat at the table and started counting money up. "Yo, Pillz, I got twenty-four five, that cool?"

"Yeah, I'll work with you. Let me get that B-love so I can count it and I'll be right back with that work for you."

J-Jumbs handed Pillz the money and walked off to the back room. Pillz walked back a few minutes later with a clear bag in his hand with half a brick inside. "Here you go, fam. That's that butter."

"Already. Be safe out here in these streets, fam. You know niggas be hating."

Pillz pulled up his shirt, showing off his .45 pistol. "And I got that act right right here for they ass." They both started laughing as J-Jumbs walked out of the trap house. Pillz locked the front door and went to put the money in the safe.

Chapter Eleven

Mase was rolling a blunt up when his phone went off. He picked up to see it was Mo'nay calling. "Yo, Mo'nay, what's up?"

"Nothing, if you ain't too busy, I want you to take a ride with me."

"Okay, that's cool. When you trying to come get me?"

"I'm on my way now. Where you at?"

"My spot."

"Okay. I'll be there in ten minutes. I'm in a black BMW."

"Cool, I'm waiting on you then." Mase hung up the phone and put the work up he had on him before waiting for Mo'nay to arrive. He looked out the front door and saw the black BMW pull up. He walked outside and got into the car.

"Damn, Mo'nay, how many cars do you have?"

"Just three. I only drive this one when I don't want people to know who I am. Look, I want to talk to you for a minute and show you something."

"Sure, what's up?"

"You see all of this." Mo'nay asked Mase as she drove him through Amityville all the way to one ten. She pulled over in the C-Town parking lot. "A-Dog and his crew is running all of this; this is where all the smokers are at. Every street and block I took you down. Look across the street, you see that new auto parts store?"

"Yeah."

"A-Dog owns it now and I know for a fact he's moving twenty kilos every ninety days."

"You right, but everywhere you took me is his side of town."

"And what is your point?"

"You want me to set up a trap on his streets?"

"No, you just need the smokers from his streets to come to yours. That's all."

"How am I going to do that when he got more work than me and already has a relationship with them?"

"You know what Ra's biggest downfall was?"

"No, tell me."

"He didn't take risks and he hid behind his shooters. That's why him and Rock was killed in the end. Everything he had crumbled down to nothing. I'm not saying he wasn't a killer. A ten year old boy can pick up a pistol and shoot someone in the face. What I'm saying is, he didn't know how to think outside the box and that was his ultimate fatal flaw."

"So, if you are telling me all of this, what exactly do you have in mind?"

"Let me ask you this. You want to drive a Honda or a Porsche."

"Shit, a Porsche, of course."

"Then, you have to take greater risks but hide your hands when you do it."

"What you getting out of this?"

"You and your crew's loyalty and a sixty-forty split. Plus, you will continue to reup with my plug."

"So, you talking about starting a war with A-Dog?"

"Yeah, but you don't have to worry about the bullets flying your way."

"What you want me to do?"

Mo'nay looked at Mase with a devilish smile on her face. "A-Dog has a son. He's only six and not many people know about the little guy. I want you to kidnap his son. I'll let it be known that you want fifteen kilos of cocaine within forty-eight hours."

"How you know he got it?"

"Let me take care of that. Just do your part when he makes the drop. We'll get seven and a half keys a piece. I'll let him know where he can pick his son up."

"You don't think he's going to come after us?"

"No, he's not going to know it's us. Plus, he's going to have bigger problems to worry about, like trying to pay back his plug's money before they come after him. Nine out of ten times, he can't. So the war you were talking about is going to be between him and his plug. With A-Dog out of work, where do you think the smokers come to, to get high? Us."

"When you trying to do this?"

"Give me a few days to put everything together. Just be ready when I call."

"Mo'nay, I like the way you think."

"If you follow my lead, Mase, within a year, you will be a real made man. I promise you that."

"I'm with you, on God"

Mo'nay nodded as she pulled off to drop Mase back off at the trap house.

**

China walked down Forty-Fifth Street with a blunt in her hand, showing off her hour glass body and flawless looks. She was most definitely a show stopper and she knew it with her long black hair and honey brown skin. Shay-Dog couldn't help but pull up on her, looking at her Apple Bottom ass.

"China, let me smoke with you, beautiful."

China looked at Shay-Dog. "Shouldn't you be smoking with me, with all the money you got?"

"Fuck it, let's match one then, ma. Come on over here."

China smiled as she walked in the yard to smoke with Shay-Dog.

"So, what you been up to, Lil' Mama?"

"Shit, just living, trying to stay out the way of the B.S."

"What B.S. you talking about?"

"Hating ass niggas and envious bitches. The story of Amityville."

"Who the fuck you telling? So, what you smoking right there?"

"That's gas pack, nigga."

"Okay, okay, I got that loud pack too." Shay-Dog smiled as he pulled the pack out to show China what he was working with. "You still stay on Forty-Second Street?"

"No, I been moved. I live in the new homes now."

"Okay baller, I see you."

"Shit me, I'm walking. So I can't be a baller. I'm not the one with the Hell Cat in the driveway."

"China, I swear you are too much for T.V. Come inside so we can smoke." Shay-Dog watched as China walked her fat bubble ass past him into the house. Before she left, he knew he was going to be knee deep in that ass.

"So, you just be chilling in here by yourself?"

You know me. I don't like a group of niggas all up in my spot. Come over here and sit next to me on the couch, sexy."

She walked over to Shay-Dog to sit next to him on the couch as he lit their blunt up.

**

"Oh shit, daddy. I didn't know how big this dick was. Take it easy with this pussy, baby."

Shay-dog laid China on her stomach and had his arm wrapped around her chest as he was breaking her pussy in with long deep strokes.

"Oohh, daddy, what the fuck? You killing me."

All you heard was China's voice echoing through Shay-Dog's house. Shay-Dog picked China up in the doggystyle position and was pulling her back to him as he gave her more long, deep strokes. Shay-Dog had his hands on her breast, pinching her swollen nipples. China dug her nails into Shay-dog's bed covers. "Shay-Dog, daddy. I'm cumming." China squirted all over Shay-Dog's wood.

"China, come suck this dick, baby girl." China used her tongue to lick all over and around Shay-Dog's dick. "Damn bad girl, lay on your back."

China did as she was told and Shay-Dog put her legs in the air so he could pound her with tremendous force. He grabbed the top of the headboard to get more leverage as he long stroked her and started to grind his dick harder and deeper inside of her. He came all over her stomach. "Damn, that pussy was wet as fuck."

China looked up at Shay-Dog out of breath and dripping with sweat as she rubbed her pussy. "Damn, you fucked the shit outta me."

"Your pussy shouldn't be this good, baby girl."

"I got to use the little girl's room, daddy."

"It's down the hall to the right, beautiful."

After cleaning herself up, she looked at Shay-Dog. "Can you drop me off at my place?"

"Yeah, I got you, baby girl."

China went outside to Shay-Dog's Hell Cat. He opened the door for her to get in.

"Where at in the new homes you staying?"

"Go into the last entrance on the right. I'm the last house on the street."

"Damn, I didn't realize how late it was. Time flew by."

"No nigga, you fucked the shit outta me for like two hours. That's where the time went."

Shay-Dog smiled as he pulled into China's driveway. As China opened up her car door, Shay-Dog grabbed her hand to stop her. "Yo, China, real talk, I'm loving your vibe, ma."

"Hold up a second and let me get something out the house for you."

"Hurry up, I got to make a run."

"Okay, Just hold on."

Shay-Dog watched as China walked to the house. He didn't see it coming until it was too late.

"Yo, Shay-Dog." When he looked up, A-Dog was shooting him point blank in the face. His body slumped over the passenger seat as A-Dog emptied the clip into Shay-Dog's body.

China ran from the front door and got into the car with A-Dog, leaving Shay-Dog dead in the abandoned houses driveway.

SAYNOMORE

Chapter Twelve

Word hit the streets like wildfire about Shay-Dog getting killed in the new homes. The streets couldn't believe it. Niggas knew how Shay-Dog got down. They just couldn't believe he got caught slipping like that. The streets ain't need to talk. They knew the bullets came out of A-Dog's gun. The beef was thick, and tension was thick in the air.

"Pillz, you heard about Shay-Dog getting bodied?"

"Word, Tuggy, but we don't need to talk about this conversation. We already know who dropped them shells into his skull."

"Yeah, but you know the streets are going to be talking."

"Nigga, that's every day. That ain't nothing new."

"You can say that twice, homie."

"Yeah, look, come help me cook this brick up. I just ran out of the other shit I had a little while ago. I need to have this shit done before our phones start ringing."

"Yeah, facts. We can't be losing no money. Let's get this shit done A.S.A.P."

**

Mase was at the bar taking shots of Cîroc, smoking a cigarette and looking at the latest news reports. "Damn, they caught that boy slipping."

"Yeah, low key, I know Dink is going sideways right now. I know he is losing his fucking mind."

"Real shit, Shawn. When you got beef like that you don't supposed to be riding in the streets dolow. A nigga got him on the blindside and pushed his shit back. Niggas ain't bulletproof and these young niggas don't give a fuck about an OG name in the streets no more.

"Yeah, you right. So, what's up? What you had to tell me?"

"I was waiting for LA to pull up, but in the next few weeks, we are going to be up, but it comes with a price."

"What type of price?"

"Shit, that can cost us out lives if it come back on us, but this is what the fuck we signed up for. We can be kings in the streets or pawns and I ain't going out like Ra."

"You know I'm down with you on whatever."

"I already be knowing, homie."

"So, who you think Rocked Shay-Dog to sleep?"

"If I had to guess I would say A-Dog."

"I was thinking Tuggy."

"Naw, Tuggy loud with his shit. Shay-Dog ain't see this coming and Pillz ain't no murder one nigga."

"Yeah, you right. Look, while we talking, I need to reup. I've got twelve Gs right now at the spot."

"Cool, let's go take care of that now."

**

"So, I want this wall to be covered from one end to the other with a display of the rims, like a showcase when the customer pulls in. I want the stereo systems and window tint samples over here. You got me?"

"Yeah, I see your vision and how you want it, A-Dog. When is the supply truck coming in with the items?"

"Today before five."

"Cool."

"Remember, you are the shop's manager. This is a detail shop. We ain't doing no oil changes, tire rotation or tune-ups. We're putting in sound systems, tinting and lacing shoes. We're players up in here, Kevin."

"I already know. Matter of fact, someone is pulling up now."

"Yeah, I know her. Let me deal with her."

"Okay. I'll go open up the other garage doors then."

A-Dog walked out of the open garage doors and up to the driver's side of a cherry red Dodge Charger.

"Oh my God, I thought that was you when I rode by."

"Kelly, how you doing? Your mother doing good?"

"She's doing really good."

"I was sorry to hear about your brother. That shit hurt me when I found out what happened to him."

"It hurt all of us. Come give me a hug. I ain't seen you in over five years."

A-Dog walked closer to Kelly and embraced her lovingly, then kissed her forehead. "So, you work here now?"

"No, I actually own the place. Matter of fact, today is the shop's Grand Opening."

"That's what's up. I'm so proud of you. You doing all good for yourself."

"I'm trying."

"Before I forget, my brother wrote you some letters before he died. My mom has then at the house. She ain't know where to send them."

"Okay. Look, I have to get back to work but I'll swing by my house and pick them up on my lunch break. I'll bring them back here for you."

"Thank you Kelly, and you know if you ever need anything you or your mother, I'm here for you."

"We know, trust me, we do."

"Okay. If I'm not here, leave them with my shop manager and he will make sure I get them."

"Okay."

Kelly gave A-Dog a hug before getting back into her car and pulling off. A-Dog watched her leave before walking back into the detail shop.

**

Mase's phone went off. He looked at the display and saw it was Mo'nay calling him. "Mo'nay, I've been waiting to hear from you. Is it time?"

"Yeah, you ready?"

"Yeah."

"Good, you still at the same spot?"

"Yeah."

"I'm pulling up outside now."

Mase walked outside and got into the black Ford Expedition.

"Damn, what' this the smash and grab truck."

"No nigga, now listen. When we pull up, walk to the front door. There's only one person in the house. Smack her in the face with the gun, let her know shit is real. Give her this number and tell her if she call the police, the boy dies. She will be watching them pull her son out of a dumpster, get me?"

"Yeah."

"Good, in that bag is gloves, mask and a hoodie. Make sure you tell her to give that number to A-Dog." Mo'nay pulled up on the street. She looked around before pulling into the driveway. Mase got out of the truck and walked to the front door. He knocked two times. When the door opened up, he smacked the woman who answered in the face with his gun and knocked her down to the floor. He smacked her in the face one more time, then bent down and told her to tell A-Dog to call the number he gave her and if she called the police, her son would die. Then, he smacked her in the face again, knocking her out cold. He walked into the son's room and found him asleep on the bed. He wrapped him up in the bed's covers and left his mother knocked out on the floor. He closed and locked the door behind him.

Chapter Thirteen

A-Dog paced the floor with his gun in his hand and tears in his eyes while Tuggy and Pillz sat watching him in silence.

"Word for word, what the fuck happened?"

"I opened the door, and I got smacked in the face with a gun. All I remember is him yelling, "If you call the police, they will be pulling our son out of a dumpster. I don't want our son to die." She cried and shook uncontrollably. "I don't want my baby to die!"

"Chill the fuck out while I make the call. "A-Dog called the number she had given him, but nobody picked up. "Fuck, no answer." A-Dog looked at the phone as it started to ring. "Yo, who the fuck is this?"

"The motherfucker who got your son. That's all you need to know."

"What the fuck you want?"

"Fifteen kilos in forty-eight hours."

"I got that shit now. Where you want it at?"

"Behind the Pathmark on Sun Rise Highway. Drop it off and get the fuck on. When I make the pickup, and everything checks out, you can get this little nigga back. Call this number when it's done."

A-Dog looked at the phone when they hung up. "Pillz, Tuggy stay here with her. I'll be right back. I have to go pick-up fifteen kilos and make a fucking drop. As a matter of fact, Tuggy come with me. Pillz, hold the spot down till we come back. I'll handle this shit, I promise."

**

"Mase, he's about to make the drop. Once he makes it, he's going to call back to let us know it's done, and you know what we just did? We killed two birds with one stone. We got fifteen bricks on the come up and took the food out of A-Dog's mouth to feed his streets. So, now the smokers have to come to yours."

"Facts."

"Once we get the work, we will drop him off on the block, make the call and that's throwing the rock and hiding your hand at the same time."

"You are a cold-hearted bitch, Mo'nay, but I see why you act like this. Don't you know there is no love in the streets and don't no one put food on your table. You go and get it yourself."

"That's the only way you going to eat. Omar ain't put anything on my table and tell me to eat. He showed me how to come up on my own." Mo'nay got up and walked to the kitchen to get a water out of the icebox.

**

"A-Dog, you think whoever did this is going to play the game right?"

"I don't fucking know but when I find out who did, I'll body they ass and whoever is with them." A-Dog pulled up at the back of the Pathmark and looked around as he dropped the two duffle bags off into the trash can. Tuggy was outside the truck with his hand on his gun looking around at everything.

A-Dog picked up the phone and called the kidnapper's number back. "Yo, the drop is made."

"I'll call you when I pick it up."

**

"You ready? He said the drop is done."

"Yeah, let's do this." Mo'nay and Mase drove to the drop off and picked up the duffle bags. "Is everything there?"

"Yeah, fifteen of them."

"Good, let's go drop baby boy off now." Mo'nay pulled up on the corner of the street where A-Dog's baby mama lived. Mase got out of the truck and walked him to the fence on the corner. "Stay right here and don't move. Your daddy is about to come get you now, okay."

The little boy nodded as Mase got back into the truck. "Make a call."

**

A-Dog looked at the phone as it rung suddenly. He picked it up. "You better have something good to fucking tell me."

"Calm the fuck down, nigga. Your little man is on the corner down the street from your baby mom's house."

A-Dog hung the phone up and ran out the door and down the dark block. He stopped running when he saw his son standing next to a fence. He ran up to him, picked him up and pummeled him with kisses.

Tuggy and Pillz had their guns out, looking around as he carried his son back home.

SAYNOMORE

Chapter Fourteen

Mase walked into the room and placed the duffle bag on the table. He looked at LA and Shawn, who was seated at the table smoking a blunt. "Pass that blunt, LA."

"Where was you last night?"

"Putting some serious work in for us."

"Shawn was telling me a little something about it but ain't get into details. He just said niggas can get smoked over it."

"Last night, I kidnapped A-Dog son and pistol whipped his baby mama."

Shawn and LA looked at Mase funny when he said that.

"I made him give me fifteen kilos of cocaine to give him back. In that duffle bag is seven and a half bricks. Plus, I got a plug now."

"Yo, you know he's about to come for a nigga head, Mase."

"Chill the fuck out, LA. He don't even know it was me, real talk. He don't know who the fuck it was. So, we good."

"So, where the other seven and a half bricks at?"

"I had to pay somebody for the hookup with those but the point is we up now and the streets is ours now. We just got to move smart, Shawn.

"So, you sure this shit ain't going to come back on us?"

"I don't give a fuck if it do. They guns blaze just like ours do and like I said, we good."

LA and Shawn nodded as Mase got up and started pulling the kilos out of the duffle bag and placing them on the table in front of them.

**

A-Dog sat at the table spinning his gun around as he took shots of Cîroc and chased them with drags of his cigarette. He took another shot as Pillz walked up to him.

"Yo, dog, we going to find out who did this shit and smoke they ass."

"Pillz, a motherfucker had enough nerve to run up in my baby mother's crib and snatch up my little man. I want more than blood for this shit."

"You think it was them Forty Dog niggas?"

A-Dog shook his head. "We done bodied four of them bitches within the last few months. The only way we are going to find out who did this shit is to find out who moving work on the block. They got fifteen kilos from me and they not just going to sit on that."

"Word came to me a while back, like three weeks ago, that Ra's old crew was moving shit on their side of town."

"I got wind of that shit too, but it wasn't nothing major. I most definitely got them on my list."

"So, what we going to do about the work we got from Manny? We still got to come up with that B-love for him. They not going to try and hear no excuses."

"We straight on that, Pillz. I still got all the bricks from him. The shit I gave them was the shit I had from the eleven kilos I had stashed before."

Pillz poured himself a shot of Cîroc as A-Dog was talking. "So, how you want to work the block now?"

"How much money we have put up to pay Manny with?"

"Like three twenty-five."

"Yo, you and Tuggy hit your people up in the boroughs and let them know we got six kilos, ninety-seven percent pure, for a hundred and eighty Gs. That will cover us with Manny. Then, we can find out who played with fire and who's going to get burned."

"Let me go take care of that right now and make the call to Tuggy."

"Pillz, we have to play broke on the block right now until the rabbit comes out and show his face."

"Copy that. I'm about to drop the bag and a bug in Tuggy's ear now."

A-Dog took another shot and started twisting his locks as he sat at the table.

Chapter Fifteen
Four weeks later.

Mo'nay picked up the phone and called Mase as she sat at the red light, looking at Shawn's new all white on white BMW droptop.

Mase picked up the phone after a few rings. "Mo'nay, what's up, beautiful?"

"I'm trying to find out why is your boy riding around in an all-white BMW like shit ain't hot right now?"

"I'll talk to that fool. He tripping."

"Just know A-Dog shut down his traps and if I know him like I think I do, he's watching the streets. Shawn is riding around with a big ass red target on his back that says *I kicked in your door*."

"I'm about to call that nigga now. I told him not to get happy and buy that shit."

"Take care of your business before somebody kick in your door and take of their business because if word get out, trust and believe, he is pulling up." Mo'nay hung up the phone and pulled off. She was now knowing she shouldn't have fucked with Mase.

**

A-Dog was looking out the window when Tuggy walked into the house. He turned around and looked at Tuggy. "What's the word on the streets?"

"Mase, LA and Shawn is eating real good on the streets. Shawn is driving around in a droptop BMW and shit."

A-Dog smiled at Tuggy before turning back to the window. "Of course he is. There is always one weak link in a group. What about LA and Mase?"

"Same old cars, no flashy shit."

A-Dog sucked his teeth and sat down as he lit his blunt and licked his lips. "What's Shay-Dog's little homie's name that was always with him?"

"You talking about, Dink."

"Yeah, where is he?"

"Word is, after Shay-Dog got bodied, son went missing in action. Nobody knows where he's at."

"We're going to give it a few more weeks. If them niggas is still bubbling, we going to pop they top. You would think niggas would lay low for a few months."

"So, we just going to let these niggas eat?"

"Yeah, let them get full and enjoy their meal on the table right now. When it's time, they gonna wish they said their prayers.

**

Mase was playing pool and smoking a blunt with LA when Shawn walked into the bar. "Yo-yo, what's good, fam?" Mase placed the pool stick down on the pool table and looked past Shawn to the car outside. "I thought I told you don't get that shit. That car hot."

"What's the point of trapping if we can't enjoy our bread and butter?"

Mase walked up to Shawn. "I took this nigga child and beat his bitch up so we can eat, not so we can be out here riding around in a hot BMW that says *I took your shit*."

"Look man, I'll park the car, but I don't know what the fuck we worried about. Like you said, our guns blaze just like theirs."

"Nigga, just because we are souljas don't mean we have to be in warfare. You don't see me or LA riding around like that."

"So, what the fuck you doing with your bread?" LA looked at him.

"Real talk, I got a house out of town where wifey stay at, and I'm still living in my old spot behind the Cloverdale's. Ain't nothing changed in my world."

"Y'all made ya point, I'll park the whip."

"Yeah, cool. Now let's talk about this money. We only have two birds left. I'm trying to pick up four of them today."

"How much we talking about, Mase?"

"A hundred and thirty-six grand will get us four. We don't need to run out. We got shit on lock right now, LA."

'Copy that. Niggas wasn't eating like this when Ra had the keys to the city."

"Because he was for himself but I'm for the team. So look, I need forty-five grand from both of you today so I can get this work before it's too late."

"Let me go get that now then."

"Big facts, LA."

"Yeah, me too."

"Cool, so I'll meet both of y'all back here in two hours?"

"Yeah."

"For sho."

"Yo, Shawn, park the car homie."

"I already told you I was in on it."

Mase dapped both of them up as he was walking out of the door to the bar. He picked up the phone and called Mo'nay to let her know what he needed.

SAYNOMORE

Chapter Sixteen

Jake opened the shop garage for A-Dog to pull his car inside. A-Dog stepped out of the car and walked up to Manny and shook his hand. "It's good to see you again. Let's go talk in my office."

"After you, Manny. It's good to see you too."

A-Dog walked into Manny's office and took a seat in front of his desk. Manny handed him a bottle of water. "So, tell me A-Dog, how is business going?"

"It's been a few bumps in the road so I closed down all my stores for now to check some things out." Manny looked at A-Dog and rubbed his chin. "What you mean you had to close down the stores? What type of bump in the road did you hit?"

"Can I smoke in here, Manny?"

"Sure, I don't mind."

A-Dog pulled out a cigarette and lit it. "About five weeks ago, someone kicked in my baby's mother's door and kidnapped my son and left a number for me to call. I called the number, and they wanted fifteen kilos from me. I paid the ransom and got my son back within twelve hours. So, I stopped all stores from opening to see who else opened up. That way I can find out who did it and pay their ass a visit."

"That was very smart what you did. You are giving them a chance to expose themselves and a fool will always do so. How long do you plan on keeping the stores closed for?"

"I think I found out who did it. One of his crew members is driving around in a white BMW."

"Like I said, the fool will always expose his hand if given a chance. What will you do now?"

"Let them think everything's blown over. I'ma act like I don't know shit. Then, I'll open up on them."

Jake opened the office door and looked at Manny and gave him a thumbs up. "So, do you want the twenty car tires for your new shop?"

"Always."

Manny nodded at Jake before he closed the office door. "A-Dog you know what I like about you? You're quiet and hungry. You are not loud at all you are going to go very far in this business but don't get comfortable with just twenty. Try thirty or even forty a pop. Remember, the goal is to get rich."

"You are right. As soon as I handle my business, we will talk about that."

"Good, I can't wait." Manny walked A-Dog to his car and watched him pull off before walking back to his office.

**

"Mo'nay, this is most definitely different. Why did you want to meet way out here in West Bumblefuck?" Mase looked around the empty warehouse. It was damp and dark inside except for the little bit of light coming through the windows.

"Because you are hot right now and I'm not going to take the chance of getting mixed up in your bullshit. A-Dog is not stupid, and he is paying close attention to the streets. Your boy riding around in a new droptop is saying everything he needs to hear.

"I checked him about that shit. He parked the car."

"And what does that mean? Eyes are already on him. Now LA was a little bit smarter, he got him a nice spot out of town and from what I hear, it's laced out from top to bottom, wall to wall.,"

"How you know about that, Mo'nay?"

"His bitch in the hair shop running her mouth off to everyone bragging. She saying my man this and my man that, but six out of ten times, A-Dog ain't going to find that out. The point is I don't need my name in no bullshit. You don't think it was funny that A-Dog had fifteen kilos and right after he paid to get his son back, he closed all his trap houses?"

"Shit, we got all of his work. That's why."

"If you think that, then you are dumb as a pile of rocks. He's watching the streets to see who is moving the work and where the crackheads are shopping at now. Who got what blocks on lock now. Just to make this clear. No, I'm not going to the bar no more and I will not be seen with you right now, Mase."

"Damn, you act like this shit was my idea. You thought of it, not me."

"You're right, I did, and I thought you and your boys would think like me and move smarter. I slipped through the cracks for seven years with Don-Killer and five years by myself on the streets. Don't nobody know my business because I don't broadcast it, Mase."

"I respect what you are saying and don't think I don't. You're right Mo'nay."

"Good, tighten up. So, you have my money?"

"Yeah, a hundred and thirty-six grand. It's right here in the bag." Mase handed Mo'nay the bag.

Mo'nay walked to the car and pulled out her own bag and handed it to Mase. "It's four in there, ok."

"Cool, I'll call you when I'm ready for a reup."

"Stay out of the eyes of the streets because they are watching everything."

Mase nodded, walked back to his car and pulled out of the warehouse.

Mo'nay knew she would have to kill Mase before her name came to the light.

Chapter Seventeen

"The real Pillz bury. What's the word?"

"Just vibing on a daily basis, Blue."

"I know you have a blunt ready to put in the air."

"You already know."

"When is the shop going to open back up?"

"In a minute. We was just checking out some shit first. Trying to see how some things played out."

"Yo, copy that. You need a light?"

"Naw, I got one, scrap. So, what them niggas talking about on the other side of town with them prices on the twenty-eight and up?"

"They raping the block. They asking for two grand on twenty-eight grams and they ain't pushing no more weight than that. I don't even know how they got on like that, but they eating real good right now."

"Pillz looked at Blue when he said that. He smoked the blunt and passed it to him.

A-Dog was pulling up into the yard.

"Yo Blue, let me bust at A-Dog. You can take that gas with you, homie."

"Peace. That's love, fam."

Pillz dapped Blue up as he walked out of the yard.

"A-Dog, tell me something good, scrap."

"Shit, let's take these blocks back, homie and get ready to push these cats wigs back."

"I've been waiting to hear that shit for too long now."

"What? Push they caps back or open back up?"

"Both."

"Come inside, I got six of them with me. Hit Tuggy up and let him know to get over here because two of them is his."

"I already texted him and let him know what it is. Let's take the block back. Matter of fact, he just hit me back. He's on the way now."

Pillz and A-Dog walked into the house. A-Dog placed the bag on the table. "So, how you want to deal with these niggas?"

"Right now, they think we don't know it was them, but the white BMW told us the answers to the questions we needed to know. We're going to open the streets back up and get some of this money back. Then, we are going to eat them niggas."

"I'm all for it. Let's eat both ways."

A-Dog dapped Pillz up. "Let's do it then, Pillz."

**

Mase walked up to LA and Shawn as they was watching the game on T.V. in LA's house.

Damn, where the fuck you been?"

"A few towns over taking care of the business."

"And how did that go?"

"We good, like always."

"So, what's that look on your face like you got something on your mind?"

"The streets talking. I'm thinking we should just eat on them now."

"Man, fuck that. Let's keep getting this money. Like you said, them boys are in the blind. We got the streets now and that's all that matters, hands down."

"You know what, LA? You're right, come on. Let's cook this shit up and get ready to put it on the block."

"Now you talking," Shawn said as he got up and walked to the kitchen.

**

"Real shit, A-Dog, we need to handle Shawn and them niggas now. They think shit is sweet with us."

"We are going to deal with them. Just not now. Now that we know who did this shit, we are going to rock them to sleep."

"Fuck it then, but it that was my little man, that nigga's mother would be in a pine box."

A-Dog ain't say a word. He just looked at Tuggy as he weighed the cocaine up on the table.

"Yo, A-Dog, don't pay Tuggy no mind. We all mad about that shit, but it's your call. So, just know we are standing by, behind you all the way."

"I already know, Pillz, real talk."

"Look, we need some more baking soda and Ziplock bags."

"I'll go make that run. I'll be back in a minute, fam."

"Cool."

"Yo, Tuggy, I'm running to the store, You good? Need anything?'

"Naw, I'm straight, bro." Pillz walked out the door and locked it behind him.

**

"Yo, Mase, ain't that that nigga Pillz over there in the Pathmark parking lot?'

"Yeah, that's that nigga. I'm about to ride on his ass!"

"Fuck it, come on then." Mase pulled up in the parking lot and LA opened the car door. With hoodies on and guns out, they ran up on Pillz. "Yo, Pillz."

Pillz turned around and saw LA and Mase running up with pistols pointed at him. He ducked behind a car as they started to shoot at him. He pulled his gun out and jumped from behind the car, shooting at LA and Mase. "I ain't sweet, nigga. What the fuck you thought?" Pillz sent LA and Mase running for cover behind different cars as his bullets flew their way. Pillz saw Mase running back to his car. He jumped from behind his cover and continued to shoot at Mase as he was running.

"Pussy ass nigga, run." He didn't see LA on the side of him, coming from the front of a parked car.

"Pillz."

When Pillz turned around, he looked at LA as he shot him three times in the side, dropping him.

LA stood over Pillz and pointed his gun at his face. LA pulled the trigger, but nothing happened because the clip was empty. He heard the police sirens coming and looked at Pillz body on the ground. He ran and jumped into Mase's car as sirens drew closer.

Mase mashed the gas and pulled off before the police arrived. "You got his ass."

"Hell yeah, I popped his ass three times. I was going to pop his ass in the head, but my clip was empty. That nigga is peter rolled. I saw when his eyes rolled to the back of his head."

"We need to park this car and get the fuck out of here before we get pulled over in this bitch."

"I got us, chill. We're about to be up out of this bitch right now."

**

A-Dog got a text to his phone from China that said *call me A.S.A.P.*, but before he could respond, he received another text from Blue that read, *call my line now bro.* He looked at Tuggy, who was looking at the text messages on his phone going off back to back. He called China. After two rings, she picked up.

"A-Dog, Pillz was just shot up. They rushing him to the hospital on the Southside now."

"What the fuck you mean he been shot? By who?"

"I don't know, A-Dog. I don't' know."

"Hell naw, Yo', Tuggy."

"I already know. I'm on the phone with Blue now. He said Mase and LA caught him up at Pathmark and clipped him good. They don't know if he's going to make it."

A-Dog hung up the phone and grabbed his gun off the kitchen table. "Come on, Tuggy. We got business to handle." Tuggy grabbed his gun and ran outside to A-Dog's truck and got in.

Chapter Eighteen

China walked into the hospital and saw A-Dog and Tuggy in the waiting room with Pillz sister. "Hey A-Dog, how is he?"

"We don't know yet. The doctor said they trying to get a bullet out of his side. If he would have got here five minutes later, he would be dead. They stopped the bleeding, but they need to get the bullet out now."

"How long has he been in there for?"

"Two hours or more."

Everyone looked up when the doors opened, and the doctor stepped into the waiting room. A-Dog and Pillz sister walked up to the doctor. "How is he doctor?"

"He's stable right now. He lost a lot of blood, but we gave him an I.V. and stopped the bleeding. He's very lucky. The bullet we just removed missed his spine by less than an inch."

"Can we see him?"

"Right now, he needs his rest. He's in ICU recovering. He will be there for a few weeks but after a little physical therapy, he should be back at a hundred percent."

"Okay, thank you, doctor."

"You're welcome."

Pillz sister turned to A-Dog. "Who shot my brother?"

"Baby girl, I'll take care of this. Call me if you need anything."

"A-Dog, please handle this."

"I will." A-Dog kissed her on the forehead and looked at Tuggy and China. "Come on, y'all, we out."

After they walked out the hospital, Tuggy looked at A-Dog. "You still want to wait?"

"We riding out tonight. Somebody is going in a body bag. My bullets don't have no names on them. If they with them, they can bleed with them."

"That's what the fuck I'm talking about."

"China, you think you can find out where them niggas is at?"

"Let me make some calls and I'll let you know something as soon as I can."

"Cool. You need a ride?"

"China, thanks for coming to check up on my nigga. That's love."

"A-Dog, you already know how we rocking."

"I be knowing already."

Tuggy nodded at China as she walked off.

**

"Now, that's how you pop a nigga. You get close up on him and let that bitch loose on him. I like how you did that shit, LA."

"You know I put that work in for the family, hands down."

Shawn walked out of the back room when he heard all the noise coming from the living room. "What the fuck is going on out here?"

Mase walked up to Shawn. "We just caught that boy, Pillz down bad and LA made sure his last bed is a slab of cold steel down at the city morgue."

"Wait, y'all niggas just killed Pillz?"

"Fucking right."

LA rolled a fat blunt and looked at Shawn.

"Where at?"

"Pathmark."

"So what about A-Dog and Tuggy then, Mase?"

"Man fuck them niggas, Shawn. They on the hit list too."

"So y'all niggas take Pillz out. The only one who just wants to make his money, smoke his weed and fuck a bitch. Who never on the bullshit. But ya'll knowing Tuggy and A-Dog is about that life for real, for real. Go get strapped up and go look for them niggas now before they catch us down bad."

"Man, fuck them dudes. They time is coming. We just got to stay low for right now. LA, you still got shit at your old spot?"

"Hell no. The only thing in there is an air mattress. That spot is a front."

"What about you, Shawn?"

"You know I'm ducked off in the cut."

"See, we good. Plus, them fools probably don't know it's us. They might think it's that Forty nigga, Dink coming back at them."

LA leaned back on the couch and put his legs up as he smoked his blunt, "Man I don't give a fuck if they do know it was us. They bleed just like anybody else."

"Look man, let's just get the fuck out of here until things cool off for a couple of weeks."

"If that's what you want to do Mase, fuck it, It's your call."

"Yeah, Shawn."

Mase dapped Shawn and LA up as they all left the trap house going their own ways.

SAYNOMORE

Chapter Nineteen

Tuggy paced the fucking floor back and forth, smoking a blunt and looking out of the window. "It's been two and a half weeks since them niggas caught Pillz down bad and we ain't do shit yet about it."

"Tuggy, you act like we know where them fools is at. We done been to the trap and all. Niggas on the block ain't seen them. They hiding right now."

"That's why I told you we should have clapped them when we had the chance. Now, those dudes is up on us twice."

"Look, Tuggy, these niggas is dead. I know it, and their time is coming, homie. We got people on the block right now looking for them."

Tuggy walked up to A-Dog and passed the blunt to him. A-Dog's phone went off. He looked and saw it was China calling him.

"China, what's up, ma?"

"I found out where that nigga, LA is living at."

"Word, how you find out?"

"His chatty wife came up in the hair salon running her mouth off about the house he got them, and a bunch of other fuck shit up in there."

"So, she told you where they live at?"

"Hell no. I followed the bitch when she left. They house is in Brootwood. I'll text you the address."

"I knew I could count on you, beautiful. You never let a nigga down."

"You know I love your ass."

"The feeling is mutual, China."

"I'm about to text you the address now."

"Cool." A-Dog hung up the phone and looked at Tuggy. "Yo, I got LA address. China came through for us. Let's go body this nigga."

"Already, let's do this."

**

A-Dog and Tuggy sat quietly in the car on the dead end road as they watched LA's house. It was seven thirty in the evening. Both of them was dressed in all black. A-Dog had a Mossberg pump fully loaded and Tuggy had two Glocks in his hands. Both of them was watching LA's house waiting for his front door to open.

"I just say we go kick in his fucking door, A-Dog and kill everyone in there.

"The only person who needs to die in house is LA and nobody else."

"Look, A-Dog, someone is coming out the house."

"Bingo, there is our guy."

"LA is a dead man!"

LA walked out of the house and lit a cigarette on the steps as he talked to Mase on the phone. He walked down the stairs to the front of the driveway, paying no attention to the black car one house over from his.

"You ready?"

"Yeah, let's do this, A-Dog." Tuggy opened the car door.

LA had his back to them, talking on the phone.

A-Dog kept his door open as he ran up to LA with the pump in his hand. "What's popping now, nigga?"

LA turned around and looked at Tuggy pointing both guns in his face. LA dropped his phone. A-Dog ran up on the side of him, pulled the trigger and released the fury rage of the shotgun's blast, blowing LA to the ground. Tuggy stood over him and unloaded both .45 into LA's face as A-Dog kept shooting his body up with the pump. LA's body was unrecognizable when they were done. Tuggy and A-Dog ran and jumped into the car and peeled off as the neighbors ran outside to see what was going on. Mase couldn't believe what he had heard on the other end of the phone.

**

Mo'nay was laying down in her down bed when her phone went off. She looked to see it was Mase calling her and put her T.V. on mute as she answered her phone. "Hello."

Mase was talking fast in a panicked voice. "We need to talk now, Mo'nay."

"First off, stop talking so fast. I can't understand a word you saying, and do you realize it's ten-thirty, right?"

Mase took a big breath before continuing. "Mo'nay, they just killed LA. We need to talk, but not over the phone. I need your help."

"Mase, I'm not getting involved in your bullshit. I told you. You and your team was moving too sloppy. Then, you tried to kill one of his boys two weeks ago and ain't even do that right. Don't call me because you fucked up. Find someone else to run to. I ain't got shit to do with this."

"Bitch what the fuck you mean you ain't got shit to do with this. It was your idea to kidnap that nigga's kid. Now that shit is coming to the light, you trying to stay in the dark bitch. I'm not going to be the only one to put work in because if A-Dog knew you set this shit up, your head would be on the chopping block too. So, you need to make a choice. What the fuck you going to do, Mo'nay?"

Mo'nay sat up in bed, not believing what Mase just said. Not only did he threaten her, but he called her a bitch. She knew he just lost his mind. "Where do you want to meet up at Mase?"

"The same spot we did the last drop off at. I'm on my way there now."

"Let me get dressed, I'll be there in thirty minutes."

"I'll be waiting."

Mo'nay hung up the phone and got dressed. Mase ain't know who he was dealing with, but he was going to find out real soon.

**

Mase sat outside the warehouse on the hood of his car, smoking a cigarette and waiting for Mo'nay to pull up. He looked down the road to see the blue light from the BMW pull up next to his car. He waited as she got out and walked up to him.

"Let me tell you something nigga. Don't you ever call my fucking phone threatening me or calling me out my name. I ain't one of them bitches in the streets you fucking. Now, what you want?"

"Fuck all that. I need you to get A-Dog to meet you somewhere so I can kill this fool."

"And how you know he will meet me somewhere?"

"I don't know that. That's your job to convince him and it's my job to lay his ass down when he get his ass there. So figure it out. That pussy just killed LA in the worst way and I ain't letting that shit ride."

"I'll see what I can do and get this shit done."

Mase ain't say a word. He looked at Mo'nay then flicked his cigarette, got back in his car and drove off.

Mo'nay just watched him as he pulled off, not knowing the line he'd just crossed.

Chapter Twenty

A-Dog walked into his detail shop to his office to find three letters on his desk from Murder postmarked five years ago. He was about to open them when he heard someone call his name. He stashed the letters in the desk drawer and then got up to see who was calling his name. When he walked through the doors, he saw Mo'nay standing there looking beautiful in her Chanel outfit. "Damn, its been a while, Mo'nay. To what do I owe the pleasure of this visit?"

"The streets is talking, A-Dog and I heard about Pillz. How is he doing?"

"He's a trooper. He took that shit and smiled."

"Okay, 2Pac number two. Give him my best wishes. I bet he's happy that you and Tuggy took care of LA last night."

A-Dog looked at Mo'nay and tilted his head at her. Before he could say a word, Mo'nay looked at him. "Like I said, the streets is talking."

"So, you giving me a heads up?"

"No, a head start so you don't get caught down bad. I would hate to hear the streets say your name with R.I.P. in front of it."

"That's love and respect, Mo'nay. Real shit. What you been up to?"

"Staying all the way out the way. How things been with you? Other than the new empire I'm standing in. I see you took my advice."

"A man should always listen to a mature woman. So yes, I did take your advice, beautiful."

"Well, take care, A-Dog and remember what I said because empires don't go to war over souljas because it is their job to die in the line of duty. Empires go to war over kings because it's their job to feed their people and lead the troops."

A-Dog just watched as Mo'nay got into her G-Wagon and pulled off after saying what she had to say.

**

Tuggy walked into Pillz recovery room. Pillz was sitting in bed eating a Jell-O cup when Tuggy walked into the room. "I know you ain't enjoying that cup of Jell-O that much, Pillz?"

"Damn, I almost got took out the game. You ain't seen me in three weeks and the first thing you say to me is about a cup of Jell-O?"

"Well, A-Dog said you was good. You told him you took them shots and smiled."

"Man, that shit hurt like hell. When I was looking down the barrel of that gun, I just knew I was dead when he pulled that trigger but the gun ain't go off. I just knew I had an angel over me. Tuggy, I'm going to kill that nigga LA, on gang."

Tuggy leaned over and whispered in Pillz ear. "Me and A-Dog killed that boy in the worst way last night. We left his body unrecognizable."

Pillz look at Tuggy and dapped him up. "So, you good to come up out of here?"

"Maybe in a couple more weeks. The doctor said they just want to keep a close eye on me for right now. Where A-Dog at?"

"On the block. You know we still got to get the plug money up. I don't mean to say this in a fucked up way but just because you got shot don't mean the world stop turning. Debts are still owed, and the clock is still ticking."

'I already know but things are looking up because I know you and A-Dog handled that business, hands down."

"With no questions asked. That's what brothers are for. So, how that Jell-O taste?"

"You got jokes?"

"Naw, but I'm glad you doing better. I just came to tell you the news. I got to go help A-Dog because not only are we pulling our weight, we're pulling yours too."

Pillz and Tuggy dapped each other up. Pillz watched as Tuggy left the hospital room. He couldn't wait to get back on the block with his home team and get back to the money.

Chapter Twenty-One

"So, what Mo'nay say?"

"She going to take care of the business and set A-Dog up for us. I want that nigga head on a table."

"So what, everything stops so we can deal with A-Dog and his boys?"

"No, we just going to work off our phones for now."

Mase took a seat at the kitchen table and rolled up a blunt. "Look, Shawn, we need to make our stomp in the streets and I just got word that Pillz ain't even dead."

"LA said he clapped that guy till his eyes rolled in the back of his head."

"Yeah, I was there. I saw it when he laid him down. I don't know how the fuck he survived that one, dead ass."

Mase passed the blunt to Shawn. "I'm about to head out. Hit me up later and watch your back out here."

"You know that already, fam." Mase walked out the doors to his car. He knew he had to kill A-Dog before it was his spirit looking down at his own body because of a slip up.

**

Shawn put the blunt out and got his car keys off the table. He knew what he had to do, and he wasn't going to end up like LA or on the run for a body. Mase was no leader, and he wasn't going to have him dead in no coffin. He pulled up to Southside Hospital and checked his gun to make sure it was fully loaded before he went inside. He walked up to the front desk.

"Hello, how may I help you?"

"Yes, I'm here to visit Anthony Ham."

"And you are?"

"His brother, Kevin Ham."

"Okay. Let me look him up. Yes, he is in room two fourteen on the third floor. You'll need this. It's your visitor's pass."

Thank you." Shawn looked around before he walked in the room. Once in the room, he closed and locked the door. He looked and ain't see Pillz on the bed. He heard the bathroom toilet flush. He turned around as Pillz was coming out the bathroom. Pillz stopped in his tracks when he saw Shawn. "I'm just here to talk, nothing else."

Pillz ain't say a word. He just looked at Shawn. Shawn waited. Pillz mean mugged him as he walked to the bed. "Then talk, nigga. What the fuck you got to say to me?"

"Pillz, I ain't have shit to do with you getting shot. I ain't even know that shit went down till Mase and LA came and told me afterwards."

"So, you telling me you ain't have shit to do with this?"

"Hell no. It's deeper than what you think. Even down to A-Dog's son getting kidnapped. Nigga was pawns and ain't know from the beginning."

"So, tell me what the fuck you mean then because I'm in the hospital with three fucking gunshot wounds that almost took my fucking life."

Look, about four months ago, Don-Killer's bitch, Mo-nay pulled up to the bar talking to Mase. Next thing you know, she blessed us with a kilo for forty Gs. Then, another one after we paid the first one off."

"So, you telling me that Mo'nay's been supplying y'all this whole time?"

"Yeah, thirty-four a brick. Cash up front but hear me out. So, one day out the blue, Mase came to tell me and LA he got a job to do for seven and half kilos. He ain't let us know what it was. About three weeks later, he popped up to the table with seven and a half keys. LA asked what he do to get them and that's when he mentioned the kidnapping of A-Dog's son with Mo'nay's help. We knew what time it was after that. Yeah, it was fucked up, but we couldn't turn our backs against Mase. Him and Mo'nay been doing too much, so after shit went down with LA, Mase called Mo'nay for a meeting. They met up and now Mo'nay is supposed to be setting A-Dog up for Mase to body him this week, I think.

"So, why the fuck should I believe you? How do I know this ain't all a setup?"

"Pillz, I don't give a fuck if you are from Albany Ave. and Smith Street and I'm from the Forties and Flat Tops. Me and you go back to blue juice. You have known me from the age of eight, playing freeze tag and living two houses down from each other. I ain't come here on no bullshit."

Pillz looked at Shawn, knowing he was right. They go way back and the story he was saying was adding up to the tee. How else would they get put on if it wasn't for Mo'nay and how did Mase know where A-Dog's BM stayed at.

"Let's just say the shit you are telling me is the truth. Why the fuck you turning against your nigga?"

Them niggas put me in warfare without letting me know what went down. I'm not trying to do life in prison and I'm not trying to be put in a grave. I'm trying to end this bullshit now."

"You got a number?"

"Yeah."

Shawn wrote his number down on a piece of paper and handed it to Pillz. "I'll check your story out. If what you say is true, I'll handle it on my end. If not, next time we see each other it's guns up."

Shawn nodded at Pillz. "Cool." Shawn walked out of Pillz hospital room quietly. Once the door was closed, Pillz bathroom door opened and Tina walked out and looked at Pillz. "Baby girl, don't say nothing that you heard here today. I have to make some calls. Come see me tomorrow night."

Tina walked up to Pillz and gave him a kiss and a hug before walking out the room. Once in the hallway, she picked her phone back up. "Mo'nay, you heard all of that girl?"

"I sure did, Tina. Thanks for calling me when you heard him say my name, girl. You know I got you when I see you."

"You know how we do, child." Tina hung up the phone as she walked out the hospital.

SAYNOMORE

Chapter Twenty-Two

Mo'nay threw rocks into Avon Lake behind Amityville High School. It was quiet and no one was around. Trees hid the lake, and it was late, close to ten at night. All you saw was a multitude of stars in the midnight sky. Mo'nay turned around when she heard footsteps coming her way.

"So, what is this place?"

"A lake with no bottom, Mase. Omar used to bring me here when I was younger, to go fishing and other things."

"So, why are we out here tonight?"

"Because you fucked up. You ran your mouth off to Shawn and LA about our business."

"What are you talking about?

Mo'nay looked at Mase and shook her head. "Being a boss nigga means not letting your souljas business become a problem for the entire empire and knowing that some shit they don't need to hear because it's not for their ears. Don-Killer understood that, so did Ra. I guess you missed that lesson, Mase."

"What's your point, Mo'nay?"

"Shawn went and told Pillz everything last night at the hospital. From me supplying you to the kidnapping of A-Dog's son."

"How do you know this?"

"I heard it word for word with my own two ears and he told Pillz about the setup with A-Dog. Now, I didn't even know you told him that. So now, A-Dog is on point thanks to you running your mouth off and your disloyal ass team."

Mase bit down on his teeth and shook his head in a sign of disgust. "I'll deal with Shawn about this."

"Yeah, do that because we was the ones holding the gun. Now the rabbit got the gun and after you deal with him, meet me back here."

"Why here?"

"Because we need to stay out of sight, Mase. We don't need nobody following us. That's why."

"Yeah, I'll go take care of Shawn. I'll call you when I'm done."

"Do that." Mo'nay turned around and finished throwing rocks into the lake.

**

A-Dog was at his detail shot sitting behind his desk, reading the letter Murder wrote him.

A-Dog, I hope this letter reaches you in the best of all wellbeing. I know shit is really ugly right now for me but there is a rainbow at the end of the tunnel for you still. I been racking my brain day after day. Shit wasn't adding up to me at all, fam. I had to put two and two together. Mo'nay set us up from the very beginning with Don-Killer. She had a video recorder in the living room when I killed Don-Killer and she stepped out of the camera shot when I killed him so she wouldn't be on tape. That's not all. Remember you took care of Rock, but she told you to make sure his gun was on him when you dropped him off. That was because he killed Omar and Pete and the police who worked for Omar was going to find that out and tell who he need to. That's how Ra got killed. They put two and two together when you did what you did. The white van had three hundred bricks inside of it. She knew this all along and had me take care of Don-Killer. Rock took care of Omar and Pete, you took care of Rock and Omar's people took care of Ra. She walked away with three hundred of them things nice and easy. Then, she knew shit would come to the light with us so she sent the video tape of me killing Don-Killer to the police, hoping they would kill me in a shootout right along with you. This bitch had all of this planned from the beginning. She' smart as hell, A-Dog. She set us all up. Just know you are my day one and it's all love but don't let this bitch walk. Think about what I said and handle the business fam, because of her this prison is my new home. I love you bro. Stay up, Murder.

A-Dog had a tear in his eye as he read Murder's letter, knowing everything he said was right. She was doing it again and there was no doubt he was going to kill Mo'nay , not just for what she did to his son but for murder too.

Chapter Twenty-Three

Shawn pulled up to the trap house and looked both ways before he opened his car door and stepped out. He walked into the house to see Mase smoking a cigarette and talking on the phone. He walked up to him and gave him a pound.

"Yo, let me call you back, baby girl."

"Who was that?"

"Kesha stank ass. What's good with you, bro?"

"Shit, I thought you said we wasn't going to trap out of here no more, bro."

"Yeah, I say a lot of shit, homie. Roll a blunt. I need to smoke."

"Cool."

Shawn pulled his gun out and placed it on the table with his cell phone. He got up and walked to the kitchen to dump the guts of the blunt into the trash can. When he turned around, Mase was standing in front of him with his own gun pointed at him.

"What the fuck you got going on, Mase?" Shawn took two steps back as he looked at the gun pointed in his face.

"So, you went to the hospital and told Pillz everything, huh nigga?"

"Man, enough is enough, bro. How many more people got to die? You've changed Mase since that bitch Mo'nay came around. You can't see she is poison. Everyone who fucks with her ends up dead like Don-Killer and Ra because she turns niggas against each other. Man, now you pointing a gun at me over her. She's poison, Mase. She is not for us."

"What you don't see Shawn is that she made us. That white on white BMW you have came from her efforts. Before her, you was walking. She put us on our feet and because of her we was eating. You fucked up and yeah, LA is dead. R.I.P. to him but he knows what came with this life. You went and told our enemies everything. You turned your back on us, not her, nigga."

"So, you going to kill me over this bitch, Mase? Me!"

"You killed yourself when you became a rat and told Pillz the move."

Shawn watched as the bullets came out the gun and hit him in the chest, dropping him to the floor. Blood ran out of Shawn's mouth and he looked at Mase as he tried to say something, but Mase shot him two more times, killing him before he could try and talk. Mase looked behind him and saw Shawn's phone going off. He picked it up and saw Pillz was calling him. He ignored the call and took two pictures of Shawn's dead body and sent them to Pillz. Then, he threw his phone on his dead body and walked out of the house.

**

Pillz looked at the pictures that came to his phone and couldn't believe it. Shawn lay in a pool of blood, dead. Pillz went back to the table and flipped it over in a fit of rage. Shawn was right. Him and Pillz went back to blue juice, freeze tag and the sandbox. It was deeper than two sides of town and some streets. He ain't have the love he used to have for him but he ain't want to see him in a box. Shawn respected their friendship and the visit to the hospital cost him his life.

**

Mo'nay sat in her BMW, getting her thoughts together, when her phone went off. She looked and saw it was A-Dog calling her. She sucked her teeth as she picked up the phone.   "Hello."

"I want you to know the next time I see you, you are a dead bitch. I promise you that. I told Murder not to trust you. I put it all together how you had me kill Rock and Rock killed Omar and Pete. From you setting up Murder to kill Don-Killer and Omar's people to murder Ra. You walked away with three hundred kilos. You think you won, huh?"

"No, boo boo. I did win. Even from having your nappy ass son taken and making you pay fifteen kilos to get him back, to putting it in Mase's and LA's head to kill Pillz, knowing you and Tuggy was going to kill one of them; even to making Mase kill Shawn for running his mouth off to Pillz. I been setting this shit up from the first day. See boo, I don't lose, and I hope you come through on your promise because if I see you, you're going to be lying next to Murder. It only took me five gs to pay a broke nigga in prison to get that done A-Dog couldn't believe what she just told him. Everyone was a piece on Mo'nay's chess board, and she was the King and Queen.

SAYNOMORE

Chapter Twenty-Four

Mo'nay was standing at the edge of the lake looking at the moonlight reflecting off the water's surface, when Mase walked up behind her.

"So, I see you really do like it here."

"I told you that before. It's my place of peace. How did your talk go with Shawn?"

"Let's just say a man who can't breathe can't talk."

"Good, do you know the difference between a murderer and a killer?"

Mase just looked at Mo'nay. "

A murderer may have killed two people, but we know for sure you can't be a murderer if you never killed anybody right. A killer kills all threats that come his way. No matter the risk. A killer don't lose sleep over a dead body, and don't have no feelings. He does what he has to do. I need you to become that killer for me. A-Dog and Tuggy are the shooters and just like our bullets have their names on them, they have bullets with our names on them as well."

"Okay, but how are we going to catch them down bad? They are always together."

"Let me deal with that. Have you heard the rumors on the streets?"

"I don't listen to rumors, Mo'nay. They just lies people tell."

"The thing about a rumor is there is always some truth to the lie. You just have to be quiet enough to hear the voice that the wind is carrying, and you will know the truth of which rumors to listen to. Don't you think it's funny that China was the last person seen with Shay-Dog before he was killed?"

"And where did you hear that from?"

"The secret voice of the wind. I also heard that she was in the hair salon the day that LA was killed."

"So, that's where you're getting your information from, a hair salon, Mo'nay?"

"I just find it funny that the day she was in there LA's wifey was talking about her new house in Brantwood and that night he gets killed. What are the possibilities that two different events that cost two people their lives involve her name?"

"So, you saying this bitch set up LA?"

"No, I'm saying what if she is the piece that's linking everything together for A-Dog. Like I said, if you listen long enough you will hear the truth in the rumors that are told. She might not have setup but I'm sure she gave up his location to his new home."

Mase had the look of rage in his eyes. "I'll kill that bitch."

"I know you will. You can find her here on Jefferson Ave. That's where she lives."

"How do you know that?"

"Sometimes, the predator becomes so comfortable they don't realize that they have become the prey; and what does a predator do? It follows the prey till it's ready to strike. She lives in a white house with a green and white fence."

Mo 'nay looked at Mase and walked off, leaving him and his thoughts next to the lake.

Chapter Twenty-Five

Pillz walked into the house where Tuggy was at the table weighing up cocaine and A-Dog was bagging up what they had cooked up already.

"Damn nigga, what's that look on your face? You look like someone done stole your puppy."

"So I'm guessing you ain't here about what happened last night, Tuggy?"

A-Dog looked at Pillz. "Naw, what happened?"

"Last night, China was killed. Her sister found her this morning. She was beat and choked to death."

A-Dog jumped up from the table. "What the fuck you mean?" He had a gun in his hand as he paced the floor in a state of rage. He was pointing at Tuggy and Pillz. "Mo'nay is behind this shit. I know she is. I want that bitch dead."

"A-Dog, don't Mo'nay move like a ghost? Nobody knows where that bitch stay at, and we been looking for her. She's a damn shadow in the dark."

"So, we need to look harder, Tuggy. Before this bitch get one of us down bad. Pillz, what's that boy name? Shawn? Hit him up and see what knows."

"That's the other news." Pillz pulled his phone out and showed A-Dog the picture of Shawn, who was shot to death. "They sent me this last night."

"Damn, shaking my fucking head, Pillz. A-Dog think about this. We know the bitch be at the Village Diner and hair salon. We just got to catch the bitch slipping, going, or coming out one of them spots. Then, we ice her ass."

"I been posted up at that diner, Tuggy. She ain't been there in a week."

"Look, I just came by to tell you the news, A-Dog. I'll get back on it tomorrow. I'm headed back to my spot, and I'll open the other trap tomorrow."

"Cool, watch your back out there, Pillz."

"Already." Pillz nodded at Tuggy as he walked out of the house.

**

Pillz was in the shower. As hot water ran down his body, he put his head under the showerhead. He had his eyes closed, letting the water relax his body. He cut the water off, stepped out of the shower, dried off, put his boxers on and wrapped a towel around his waist. He walked into his bedroom, sat down on the bed, and rested his hands on his head.

"It looks to me like you have a lot on your mind, Anthony."

Pillz jumped up when he heard the sound of Mo'nays voice. He looked at his night stand for his gun, but it was gone. He looked at Mo'nay, who raised up her shirt and showed him his pistol.

"Don't worry, Anthony. I ain't come to kill you. I came to talk. If I wanted you dead, I would have got you in the shower."

"What do you want to talk about?"

"Anthony, I have no problem with you. Honestly, I like you. I respect how you move and how you carry yourself."

"Let me get this right, you broke into my house just to tell me you like the way I move and how I carry myself?"

"Yeah, I did."

"Mo'nay, if you're here to try and get me to roll on my team, I'm not. They are my partners and I stand on loyalty, hands down."

"Mo'nay laughed when he said partners. "Is that what you think you are? Partners? You are not A-Dog's partner. I'm willing to bet you have never seen or talked to the connect. You probably only see five kilos at a time when A-Dog brings them to be cooked up and broke down. Murder was his partner. They did everything together. He knew the count of every brick and dollar that was in the safe."

"So, you in here to put a battery in my back and string me along like I'm your toy puppet?"

"Anthony, I don't need a puppet and I already have a toy soulja. What? You think A-Dog has love for you because he killed LA? No nigga, that was about respect. You kill my cat; I'll kill your dog. Don't get it wrong, Pillz. You are just a toy soulja and you just don't see it."

Pillz looked at Mo'nay and in the back of his mind, he knew a lot of what she said was really true. "So, what happens now that you've made your point?"

"I'm trying to give you a chance to be a top dog. When Don-Killer was alive, he gave me heaven, but I was a servant. So, I had him killed. Now, I'm in hell, but I'd rather be a ruler in hell than a servant in heaven. My number didn't change. It shouldn't be hard for you to get it. And tighten up. I followed you from Northwest Preschool by your trap house all the way to your house. You ain't lock your front door or anything. Plus, you left your gun out. You would have been an easy victim for me."

Mo'nay took the clip out of Pillz gun and dropped it on the floor. Then, she cocked it back and took the bullets out of a chamber. She dropped the gun on the floor and kicked it under the bed. "Get my number and call me when you are ready to be a ruler and not a servant."

Pillz watched as Mo'nay walked out of his bedroom. He closed his eyes and took a deep breath because he just knew he was dead.

**

Mase picked up his phone and saw the time was eleven-thirty p.m. He had been calling Mo'nay for the last hour and a half and she wasn't picking up the phone. He placed his phone down on the car seat. That's when he heard it vibrating. He looked to see Mo'nay was calling him back. "Yo, Mo'nay, I been calling you for the last hour and a half. Are you good?"

"Yeah, I was busy, and I had my phone ringer off. I had to pay attention to what I was doing. You know how it is. One slip up can cost you your life."

"What you was doing?"

"I followed Pillz and caught him off guard."

"So, you sent him on his way to the next life?"

"No, I put a bug in his ear and gave him something to think about."

"What?" You should have clapped him. That would have been one less nigga to worry about."

"Yeah, you're right or he could be a help to us. We can kill A-Dog and Tuggy from the inside."

"That's a hell of a gamble."

"Isn't life a gamble? I heard about your activity the other night too. Don't you think a bullet would have did the trick faster?"

"Yeah, but that was personal. I wanted her to feel every inch of pain before she died."

"I understand. Look, I have one more stop to make. I will call you tomorrow afternoon."

"Cool, I'll be waiting on your call."

Mo'nay hung up the phone and pulled up in the C-Town parking lot where a skinny black man walked up to her car door. She unlocked it and he got inside.

"Hey, I didn't know if you was coming or not."

Mo'nay looked at the crack head with his dirty clothes and yellow teeth. "If I told you I'll be here, I'll be here. So, here's the deal. I have a thousand dollars for you. All I need you to do is go inside that detail shop right across the street and set it on fire. Come back right here and get your money. Deal or no deal?"

Mo'nay looked at him as he stared at the wad of bills she had in her hand.

"Deal."

"Good." Mo'nay reached in the backseat, pulled out a gallon of gas and handed it to him. "Do you need a match?"

"No, I have some."

Mo'nay watched as he ran across the street and disappeared behind the detail shop. Twenty minutes later, flames appeared in the windows of the garage doors and were raising high. Then, the skinny crackhead ran across the street and jumped inside Mo'nay's black BMW. Mo'nay watched as the flames went through the roof of the detail shop before she pulled off. "Thank you, sir. Here's my end of the deal." Mo'nay handed him the wad of bills. So, where would you like me to drop you off at?

"Somewhere off of Sun Rise Highway."

"Sure, so what's over there this late at night?"

"Tuggy's new spot. He got the best prices in town."

"Oh, okay." Mo'nay dropped him off in front of Tuggy's new trap spot and pulled off. It was one A.M. by the time she made it home.

SAYNOMORE

Chapter Twenty-Six

A-Dog sat in the front of his detail shop just looking at what the fire had done to everything. He couldn't believe this. He knew Mo'nay was behind this. He locked his car up and drove off. He needed the streets to talk, so he put a kilo on Mo'nay's head, dead or alive. He didn't give a fuck no more. He just needed this shit to end now. He pulled out his phone, called Tuggy and told him to meet him at the trap spot now.

**

A-Dog walked into the hair salon and looked at all the women getting their hair done, gossiping and waiting to see a stylist.

"Look what the wind blew in. What's up, Adem?"

"What's good, Kimberly, how you been?"

"I been good, just making it. So, what brings you by?"

"Just showing some love to the shop and looking to get some love in return."

"What you mean?"

"How many of these women are getting their hair done today?"

"Well, all of them, Adem."

"So, how much is that?"

"Somewhere between six and seven grand."

"Cool, I got this."

Kimberly watched as A-Dog walked to the middle of the shop floor.

"Ladies, ladies, look, I'm showing some love today. If you are here to get your hair or nails done, it's on me."

Everyone looked at A-Dog as he handed Kimberly ten thousand dollars.

"That's me showing love to you up in here today, but I need some love back too." A-Dog pulled out another knot of hundreds. "I have twenty grand here for whoever can tell me where Mo'nay is at. I'm leaving my number right here on the counter. Call me and let me know what's good and get paid." A-Dog walked up to

Kimberly and gave her a kiss on the cheek. "You can call me any time you want, day or night, beautiful."

"Goodbye, Adem. Boy, you are too much." Kimberly patted A-Dog on the back as he walked out the hair salon. "Ladies, this is a hair salon, not 1-800- Tell on a bitch. If you want to get in touch with A-Dog, you have to find your own way as far as this number goes."

Everyone looked as Kimberly set the piece of paper with A-Dog's number on it on fire and put it in the ashtray. "Ladies, let's stay ladylike. Ain't no rats up in here."

**

Tuggy pulled up to Pillz' trap and walked in the door.

Pillz pulled the gun out on him.

"Pillz, what the fuck you got going on?"

"My bad, Tuggy, I'm just a little on edge right now."

"What the fuck happened?"

Tuggy walked into the house and sat down at the table as Pillz closed and locked the door.

"Last night, Mo'nay caught me all the way down bad. She had my gun and all nigga."

"How the fuck did that happen?"

"She followed me from the trap last night. When I got out of the shower, she walked up to me with my gun in hand. There wasn't a thing I could do but listen and hope not to get shot."

"So, what did she want?"

"The bitch tried to get me to roll on you, trying to put a bunch of bullshit in my head. That's all. Then, she emptied the clip out of the gun, took the bullet out of the head and slid my shit under the bed before walking out the house all calm and shit."

"Shit is getting too real homie with this bitch, Mo'nay. A-Dog's detail shop went up in flames last night, she's up in your spot, she had China bodied, the nigga Shawn got clapped because of her, and who knows what else she's responsible for. We beefing with a bitch that we really need on our team."

"Dog, who the fuck you telling? We need to tighten up or we're going to be the next ones with an R.I.P. over our pictures on a T-shirt."

"What you think? We need to have a heart to heart with this bitch?"

"Tuggy, I don't trust her. We just need to find a way to kill this bitch and her toy soulja, Mase."

"We will figure this shit out later, but I brought this shit by for you. A-Dog told me to drop it off."

Tuggy reached in his bag, pulled out two bricks and placed them on the table. "He said hit him up when you're done."

Pillz looked at the kilos and thought about what Mo'nay said to him last night. "Cool, say no more. I'll hit him up when I'm done."

"Pillz, be on point, homie. I don't want to get a phone call saying you got bodied."

"Likewise."

Tuggy dapped Pillz up as he walked out the door.

SAYNOMORE

Chapter Twenty-Seven

Mo'nay looked at her phone to see that Tina was calling her.

"What's up, girl?"

"Guess where I'm at?"

"I don't know. Tell me."

"I'm in the hair salon. A-Dog walked up in here and paid for everyone to get their hair done. Then, he said he got twenty grand to tell him where you were at. He left his number on the counter."

"Are you for real, child?"

I'm so for real right now, Mo'nay."

"And what did Kimberly do?"

"She waited till he left and burned the number before anybody could get it. Then, she said that her salon wasn't 1-800- Tell on a bitch and if any bitch wanted his number, they would have to get it another way."

"That's my bitch. Thanks for the heads up, girl."

"Always, you know I got you."

Mo'nay hung up the phone, called Mase and told him to meet her at the warehouse. If A-Dog wanted to put money on her head, she could do the same thing too, but with a little more dirt in the mix.

**

A-Dog, I made that drop to Pillz, but we need to talk, fam."

"What's on your mind, Tuggy?"

"Me and Pillz been talking. We need to dead this beef with Mo'nay. Too many people are being killed. We ain't making money and niggas is walking on eggshells."

"So, what you trying to say, Tuggy?"

"We need to have a sit down with Mo'nay and kill this drama before one of us end up laying in a pool of blood.

"Tuggy, do you hear yourself?"

"Yeah, I do. This bitch had Don-Killer bodied, Ra bodied, Omar and Pete bodied, China bodied. The only one we knocked off was LA after they hospitalized Pillz. She just burned your detail shop down and had Pillz at gunpoint last night. This bitch is always one step ahead of us. I'm just thinking for the good of the team.

"Look, always remember, it ain't no sit down with me and that bitch. She had Murder killed. It's up to us to settle this shit because it sure ain't going to settle itself."

"Yeah man, whatever."

"What, Tuggy? You ain't feeling it?"

"I'm just saying. What we been doing ain't working. We need to try something different. We ain't been making no bread really. We in a war and we are losing. Shit, I'm just saying."

"Name one empire that ain't lose souljas in a war. Nigga we kings. Souljas die every fucking day. How many souljas did the U.S. lose in the Japan War in Midway? Or the Korean War? Or the Vietnam War? Niggas like us get assassinated like Lincoln, Alexander, and Kennedy. You think I'm worried about a bum ass bitch?"

"You never know. That bum ass bitch might be doing the same thing that them motherfuckers who assassinated kings and presidents did. We need to move smarter before we end up like them motherfuckers."

"Look, I just put twenty Gs on her head in the hair salon and I told the niggas on the block I got a brick on her head, dead or alive. The whole hood is going to be looking for that bitch."

"Didn't you say she knocked Omar off for three hundred kilos?"

"Yeah."

"So, we better hope she don't have the hood behind her." Tuggy looked at A-Dog and dapped him up before walking back out of the door.

"Yo, you just got here where you going?"

"To see my people. I just got that feeling."

A-Dog didn't say anything as Tuggy walked to his car.

**

Mase pulled up to the warehouse and Mo'nay opened the back garage door so he could pull in. She closed the doors once his car was inside.

"I just got to ask you, Mo'nay. Do you own this spot?"

"Yeah, it's one of my many properties."

"Damn, okay, I see you, Mo'nay."

"So tell me, what the streets are saying?"

"A-Dog put a brick on your head so you might have the whole city looking for you."

Mo'nay just smiled to herself as she leaned against her car. "Yeah, and he told the ladies at the beauty salon he got twenty grand for my whereabouts today. I guess I'll have to put this dog to sleep."

"What's the plan?"

"I need shooters. Matter of fact, I know what I need to do."

"And what's that?"

"I need to make a phone call to one of Omar's old friends. Stay ducked off until I call you. I'll show A-dog the difference between long money and short money. Make sure you are on standby when I call you to meet up with me."

"I'll be waiting for your call, Mo'nay.

SAYNOMORE

Chapter Twenty-Eight
Three weeks Later.

Mo'nay stood by the edge of the lake listening to the crickets when Mase walked up on her.

"You made your call to Omar's?"

"No. Something else came across my table."

"And what was that?"

Mo'nay turned around and looked at Mase. "You have a warrant out for your arrest. You are a suspect in two homicide cases."

"What you talking about?"

Mo'nay pulled out her phone and handed it to Mase with the newspaper pulled up. She looked at Mase as he read the article about himself. He looked at Mo'nay and handed her back the phone.

"They got your D.N.A. out of China's fingernails. I'm guessing she put up a fight and scratched you before you killed her. As for Shawn, you took a picture of the dead body with his own phone and sent it to whoever and dropped the phone on his dead body, leaving your fingerprints on the phone. How fucking smart was that Mase? You didn't have gloves on?"

"Shit, what do I do now?"

Mase, you have two murder cases over your head. What can you do? Your team fucked up; you fucked up. There's no beating this shit in court. D.N.A. and fingerprints at two different crime scenes, Mase. You dropped the ball. Now, it's going to cost you."

Mase walked to the edge of the lake and looked stressed with both hands on his head. When he turned around, Mo'nay had a black .380 pistol with a silencer on it pointed at him.

"Mo'nay, what the fuck?"

"I can't trust you. I didn't know what you had going on as far as fucking up at first, but now I don't know what you might say if the police catch you." Mo'nay shot Mase two times in the chest, dropping him to the ground.

Mase looked up at her as he was taking short shallow breaths.

"You see the gloves I have on, Mase? That's because I need your phone. My number is in it, and I don't want my fingerprints on it."

Mo'nay reached down and took Mase's phone out of his pocket. She pulled his sim card out and broke it in half. She looked down at Mase, pointed her gun at his head and pulled the trigger, making sure he was dead. She rolled his body into the lake and pushed it off with a stick from the edge of the lake. Then, she walked back to her car.

**

Tuggy was watching the news while Pillz and A-Dog were smoking and playing cards at the table. "Yo, y'all come check this out." Pillz and A-Dog walked up to Tuggy as he watched the news.

"Look what they talking about."

"Police found Willy Daverson's body floating in Avon Lake today. He was shot two times in the chest and once in the head. Authorities say the body's been here for over twenty-four hours. Willy Daverson was the suspect in two homicides committed earlier in the year."

Tuggy cut the T.V. off. "That's that boy, Mase floating in Avon Lake."

"Tuggy, you sure?"

"Hell yeah, A-Dog. I went to school with that nigga."

"You think Mo'nay had him killed?"

"You know what, Pillz, I wouldn't put it past her at all. She probably didn't trust him in court and had him bodied."

"Real talk, A-Dog."

Pillz looked at Tuggy and A-Dog as they dapped each other up and talked shit about Mase. "Yo, I'm about to head out. I'll pull up on you later."

Tuggy and A-Dog nodded at Pillz as he walked out of the door.

Chapter Twenty-Nine
Three months later.

"We back on top. Money flowing and bitches on deck. We popping bottles and niggas know who we are."

"Fucking right, Tuggy. We bosses up in this bitch."

Pillz was bobbing his head, looking at the women moving on the dance floor. The club was lit.

"Pillz, what's on your mind, my nigga?"

"It ain't nothing, A-Dog."

A-Dog sat next to Pillz and started rolling a blunt. "Now, talk to me, my nigga."

"I've been down with you for a minute, even when Murder was in the picture. I done put bitches on ice, and all. You pulled up on me saying we partners but I never met the plug, and you keep dropping one and two packs off on me like I'm one of your workers. You talking about love on the price. I'm just not feeling it, homie."

"Nigga you eating, and your pockets are heavy, right? What the fuck you bitching about, nigga because you ain't meet a plug. It sounds like you trying to back door a nigga."

"Nigga, you sound crazy as fuck. As a matter of fact, you can have this shit. I'm done with your world, nigga."

"You're right. This is my world and if you done with it, you can bounce, nigga."

Pillz got up and walked out of the V.I.P.

"Yo A-Dog, what's up with Pillz?"

"Man, on Murder, fuck that nigga. He ain't part of the team no more."

"Didn't you just give him that work?"

"Not yet and I'm glad I didn't. That nigga mad because he ain't met the plug. How that fucking sound?"

"Man, fuck him. That nigga talking reckless homie. I'm eating over here. There's bottles of Ace of Spades and they doing the talking for me."

"Fucking right."

A-Dog watched Pillz as he walked out of the club doors. He looked and shot a bird at his back.

**

It had been two weeks since Pillz said fuck A-Dog. He was at Peterocan Park sitting on a bench smoking a blunt when a black BMW pulled into the parking lot. Pillz watched the car for twenty minutes before the door opened up and Mo'nay stepped out. Pillz was on his phone as she walked up to him. He pulled his gun out, sat it on his lap and looked at her. Then, he looked around to see who she was with.

"I'm by myself, Anthony. Just saw you sitting here, and I decided to stop by and pay you a visit."

"Yeah, for some reason, people you pay visits don't leave or wake up."

"You ain't go to sleep during the last visit we had. Can you put your gun up so we can talk?"

"Do I have to worry about you pulling one out on me when I put mine up?"

"Anthony, I wouldn't do that. I watched you for twenty minutes before I walked up to you. I'm not here on the bullshit. I really just came to talk to you."

"Have a seat and let's talk."

"Not right here, this is too in the open for me. My car is right over there. Come take a ride with me, Anthony."

Pillz looked around and back at Mo'nay. He knew if she wanted him dead, he would be dead. She caught him slipping twice already."

"Where you taking me?"

"We just riding around Amityville. Are you worried?"

"No, come on." Pillz walked to Mo'nay's BMW and got inside.

"Mo'nay, this car is raw as fuck. I like your style."

"Thanks, look who's coming down the street."

Pillz looked and saw A-Dog and Tuggy riding down the block in A-Dog's black Range Rover.

"That's why I told you the park is too open for me. The new kings of the Ville riding around too much for me. They want everyone to see them. That's bad for business."

Mo'nay pulled out of the park and headed towards one-ten.

"So, this is what you do, just ride around in your BMW all day?"

"No Pillz, I do a lot more."

"Like what, Mo'nay, ?"

Mo'nay pulled up at a gas station. Pillz looked around.

"You and A-Dog built this shit up from the bottom. I was there and saw it all. He only got Tuggy because he's trigger happy. That's all. You was the mind that got all the smokers to come to the spaceship, not A-Dog. He just got the plug, and how does he repay you? By saying fuck you and disrespecting you in the club in front of everyone. You speak about loyalty but look at everybody you all have crossed out to get to where you're at today. Where is your loyalty at?" Mo'nay looked at Pillz. "Let's go for a ride somewhere else." She pulled up in a cemetery and drove to her sisters grave.

"Come on, get out."

"Who is this?"

"The love of my life, my best friend, my sister, and my heart. She would have been twenty-seven this year. Trap and Murder killed her like she was a thug in the fucking street all because Don-Killer paid them to do it. She was just a baby. So yeah, I had Don-Killer killed, as well as his boy, Murder for the part he played in it."

"What about Omar and Pete? Why them?"

"Omar made me get with Don-Killer. He made me watch over his drugs. Do you know how it feels to be fucked by a different man whenever you are told to do it? I was sixteen years old, fucking old, fat, white men. When I refused, he beat me. He couldn't really love me, but he called me his child, but I was more like a slave. He never touched me, but it doesn't matter because all of his friends did. I got punched in my face and beat with chains. I just wanted to make sure I got something out of it for all the years of abuse."

"Damn, I didn't know that was your story."

"A lot of people don't. You are the first person I have talked to about this ever, but there is always a happy ending to a fucked up beginning."

"I feel your pain, Mo'nay."

"Come on, Pillz, let's get out of here and get something to eat."

"Yeah, I'm hungry as fuck. So, where we going to eat?"

"I'll take a walk out on a limb with you, Pillz. Let's call it a walk of faith."

"What does that mean?"

Mo'nay just smiled at Pillz as she drove off.

**

"Yo Tuggy, we're out here getting money, fucking bitches and we eating. My nigga, we riding good and living good; This is our shit."

"Man, pass that fucking blunt. You doing all that talking. We know the block is ours."

"A-Dog, shit so crazy. I went by Pillz' spot the other day and the trap was empty. I hit his jack but he never clapped back, so fuck him. We bubbling without him, dead ass."

"Real talk, Tuggy. What you pull this week?"

"Close to eighty Gs."

"Yeah, and Pipe came up on this shit. We have seven kilos of our own shit put to the side, Tuggy."

"Word? We just got to open another trap and we good."

"Yeah, dead ass. Look, I'm about to pull up on this little jump off I met at the club last week. She thick as fuck. I can't wait to see what that wet wet is about, hands down."

"Nigga your dick is going to fall off from fucking all them random ass bitches."

"Yeah, alright nigga. I hear you."

**

Pillz looked at the big white house with the gated fence. It had a white G-Wagon and black Lexus in the yard. There were two big Rottweilers in the front yard. Mo'nay pressed a button on her key chain and the gates opened up for her. Pillz just looked as the gates closed, and the dogs sat down while Mo'nay pulled into the yard and up to the house's front door.

"You ain't afraid of dogs are you?'

"No."

"Good, come on and get out."

Pillz opened the passenger side door and stepped out, following Mo'nay as she patted her dogs and murmured to them like babies. Once in the house, Pillz couldn't believe how laced out it was. "Damn, Mo'nay, you are on your hot girl shit, ain't you?"

"Why you say that?"

"Look how you living."

"Shit, a girl got to do what a girl's got to do."

"So, this is where you bring your niggas?"

"One, I don't have any niggas. Two, you are the only person I have ever brought here. I don't bring niggas or bitches to my house."

"So, why am I here?"

"Beats the hell out of me, but for some reason, I trust you, Pillz. The remote control is on the living room table. I'm going upstairs to change clothes. I'll be right back."

Pillz watched as Mo'nay went upstairs. He sat down on the couch and waited for her to come back down while he watched the news. He couldn't believe he was in Mo'nay's house watching T.V. Mo'nay came back downstairs in a gray sweatsuit with pictures of Bugs Bunny on them and some matching socks.

"Come into the kitchen with me, Pillz."

"So, you're going to make me some food?"

"Unless you want to cook for me yourself, then yes, I am."

"Word, what you making?"

"Don't worry. Whatever I make you are going to eat, trust me."

"I know I can trust you, Mo'nay."

Mo'nay smiled and walked up to Pillz with a spoon of food in her hand.

"Here, taste this and tell me what you think."

Pillz opened up his mouth to taste what Mo'nay had made. "Damn, that shit is good as hell."

"I told you that you would like it." Mo'nay smiled as she walked back to the stove. She made her and Pillz a plate of food as they sat at the table and talked. "Pillz, why don't you drive."

"I was saving my money up to make sure my people are good, just in case a rainy day comes."

"I like that. You reached a higher level on your own. Are you ready to be a ruler?"

"If I'm the ruler, what does that make you?"

"I'm the overseer that makes sure everything is going as planned."

"You know A-Dog and Tuggy got the hood on lock right now."

"Let them have Amityville, I've got us Pillz."

"Cool."

Chapter Thirty
One year Later.

"Tuggy, Red Flame is going to be lit tonight. Big facts. It's two hundred dollars just to get in the door. They calling it Baller Night."

"You know I'm going. Do you think that nigga who took over the Dance and Shore is going to be there?"

"Real shit, I don't know but I heard he got some money and some niggas from the Ville shopping with him now."

"Yeah, he call himself Dope Boy, but word is it's the homie, Pillz."

Look Tuggy, who is his plug? That nigga came up fast almost overnight."

"Yeah, plus niggas know who the real dope boys are in the hood. Let's ride out, we got V.I.P seats waiting for us."

Red Flame was live. There were big booty bitches, rap artists, singers, NBA players and dope boys everywhere. Red Flame was lit. Tuggy and A-Dog were upstairs in the V.I.P. popping bottles right across from a few players from the Brooklyn Nets. Tuggy stood up with a bottle of Ace of Spades, dancing to Money Bag Yo's Bag's Make it Hard, featuring Future. He looked and saw a group of people walking in the club. One of them had a black fur coat and diamonds on his neck, glistening like tiny droplets of water. The waitress walked up and gave him a bottle of Cîroc. He had a bad bitch on his side who was turning heads as she walked in the club beside him.

"Yo, A-Dog, am I tripping or is that Pillz and Mo'nay that just walked in here together on some booed up shit?"

"Tuggy, you ain't tripping. Yeah, that's that nigga and that bitch."

The DJ gave a shoutout. "Big ups, we got Dope Boy in the building."

Pillz pointed at the DJ booth showing some love.

"Yo, I know that's not who everybody is calling Dope Boy, A-Dog."

Pillz looked at Mo'nay. "You did that, didn't you?"

"What, Pillz?"

"Had the DJ give me a shoutout."

"Sure I did. I also gave the waitress three hundred dollars to convince the DJ to do that. Everywhere you go, your presence will be known." Mo'nay looked up and saw Tuggy and A-Dog looking down at them. She took her hand and placed it on Pillz' chin, turned his face towards hers and kissed him on the lips in front of everyone.

Pillz looked at her when they were done. She never did that before. "What was that for?"

"Because tonight is about business, and I don't need no other bitches distracting you. So tonight, you are booed up with me."

Pillz kissed her back. "Cool, tonight you're the boss, Mo'nay."

"Good, now let's go to our V.I.P. seats."

"A-Dog, I just ain't see that, did I?"

"Dead ass, you did. Come on, let's go say what's up."

Pillz was sitting down talking to Mo'nay when Tuggy and A-Dog walked up. Pillz looked up at A-Dog and Tuggy and stood up.

"I see you doing good for yourself."

"I am. I can see y'all are too." Pillz grabbed Mo'nay's hand and pulled her to him. Then, he wrapped his arm around her waist pulling her to him. She wrapped her arm around him as well, pulling him closer.

A-Dog just looked at Mo'nay and Pillz.

"Yo, hand me one of them bottles of Cîroc."

When Pillz got the bottle, he handed it to Tuggy.

"Love is love, right?"

"Always, Pillz."

Tuggy tapped A-Dog on the shoulder. "Enjoy the rest of y'all night."

"You too."

Pillz watched as they left the table, heading back to their section.

"Why you pull me up, Pillz?"

Pillz looked at Mo'nay. "To let them know who I am standing next to and who is on my side."

Mo'nay couldn't help but to kiss Pillz one more time.

"A-Dog, can you believe this weak ass nigga?"

"Tuggy, he's dead to me. He walking around with that bitch on his hip knowing she had Murder killed."

"Well, I guess we know how he became the new plug now." A-Dog rolled up a blunt and looked at Pillz and Mo'nay talking with people and taking pictures like they were Jay-Z and Beyonce. The look of that shit made him sick. "Tuggy, that nigga Pillz is a disloyal ass nigga, hands down."

"Man, fuck them. We balling out tonight, homie. We will deal with them another day."

"Yeah, you right."

"Pillz, come on. We have to go to the back room for our meeting." Pillz got up with Mo'nay and followed her to the back of the club. Mo'nay knocked on the door two times before it opened.

"Mo'nay, Dope Boy, come in."

"What's up, Chad."

"I was just waiting on you two to show up. So, tell me you got what I need, Dope Boy?"

"Always. I brought four of them. That's a hundred and eighty Gs. Plus, another hundred and twenty Gs for the delivery."

Chad handed the money to Mo'nay.

"Chad, call me when you're ready for me again."

"I will."

Pillz and Mo'nay walked out of the club's back door to their car.

"Mo'nay, you want to drive?"

"No, you can."

Pillz opened the door for Mo'nay, closed it after her and walked around the back of the BMW to the driver's side. He saw A-Dog a few cars down looking at him.

"Yo, Pillz." A-Dog pulled out his gun and started to shoot at him. Pillz ducked behind a car. Pillz saw Tuggy running his way and shot at him also. When Tuggy ducked for cover, Pillz jumped in the BMW and pulled out of the parking lot. He looked over at Mo'nay, who was leaning forward in pain. She had been shot in the shoulder. "Mo'nay, you good?"

"Yeah, he hit me in the shoulder."

"Fuck, I'll kill them pussy ass niggas. On god, I will." Pillz drove like a bat out of hell to Southside Hospital and got Mo'nay checked in.

Chapter Thirty-One

Mo'nay opened her eyes to see Pillz sitting in a hospital room chair beside her bed. He was asleep. Her shoulder was sore, and her mouth was dry. "Anthony."

Pillz opened his eyes at the sound of Mo'nay's voice. "What's up beautiful, how you feeling?"

"Thirsty."

"Let me get you some water." Pillz got up and gave Mo'nay a cup of water. "Here you go, Let me go get the nurse for you."

Pillz walked out of the room and got the nurse for Mo'nay. He watched as the nurse talked to Mo'nay. A few seconds later, the doctor walked into the room. Within the hour, Mo'nay was discharged from the hospital as Pillz drove her home.

**

A-Dog, what the fuck was that about last night? I thought I told you to leave that shit alone."

"Man, fuck that shit. That's a disloyal ass nigga. I just couldn't let that shit ride like that."

Tuggy looked at A-Dog as he laid back on the couch, still hung over from last night. "We been eating with no bullshit for a whole year while this nigga been M.I.A. Now, we back on this beef shit over nothing."

"Man, stop bitching. Me and you both know Pillz don't want no smoke."

"It's not about Pillz, it's about Mo'nay. One thing you're forgetting is that's not Pillz no more. His name is Dope Boy and we don't know who the fuck he is now. Remember that, killer."

"Yo Tuggy, I got a mean ass hangover and I really don't want to hear this shit right now, fam. Fuck that nigga. We run this shit and the hood know this."

"Yeah, I hope you are right because we ain't the only ones who got money now. Everybody is eating. You clapped at a plug last night and his crazy ass bitch."

Tuggy looked at A-Dog, not paying him no mind. He shook his head and walked out the front door, knowing the bullshit that was going to come their way now.

**

Pillz looked at Mo'nay laying in the bed and the type of hate he had for A-Dog and Tuggy was kill on sight, hands down! Just knowing she was in pain because of them pissed him off.

"Pillz."

"Yeah, Mo'nay." Pillz was sitting on the edge of the bed, looking at Mo'nay.

"I don't want you to do nothing to them niggas. I got this, okay?"

"Mo'nay, you talking crazy as fuck. I got this. Them motherfuckers are going to pay."

"Pillz, you are boss nigga now, and bosses don't get their hands dirty. They let other motherfuckers do the work for them."

"Mo'nay, this is personal, and some shit a nigga just got to take care of himself. You been holding me down for a year plus. Now, let me do my part by holding you down."

"Anthony, you really do love me, don't you?"

"You fucking right I do. With no questions asked."

"Then promise me one thing."

"And what's that?"

"That you won't let them kill you."

"You got my word, Mo'nay. I promise you that queen." Pillz got up and walked out the room with murder on his mind. The first thing he was going to do was pull up on Tuggy the strong way and let him know shit was real. He knew exactly how he was going to get his message across to them.

**

Monica opened her front door, walked into the house and was thrown into the living room wall. She looked up and had a gun in her face.

"Easy, chill for a second, Monica. I don't got no smoke with you but I will kill your ass to deliver a message to Tuggy. Let him know it's guns up and play time is over. I'm not going to hear about this from the police, right?"

"No, no."

"Good, because if I do, I'm going to come back and not just for you but your whole fucking family tree. Come on y'all, let's roll out."

Monica slid down to the floor, still shaking from what just happened.

**

Tuggy walked into the house. Monica was hiding in the bedroom when he walked in there. She had a baseball bat in her hand.

"Monica what's wrong?"

"Pillz was in our house, Tuggy. They put a gun to my fucking head and threw me to the wall like I wasn't shit. I thought I was going to die. Pillz told me to tell you play time is over. He threatened my whole family, Tuggy. He told me he would kill my ass just to make a point to you. What the fuck did you get me and my family into?"

"Monica, I'll take care of this. I got this. Trust me, bae, I got this."

"Got what, Tuggy?" I could have been killed today over your bullshit. Pillz and them goons was in my damn house waiting for you to walk through the door, Tuggy. Just get out. Get out!"

"Monica, please."

"Tuggy, get out. Just leave, please. Get out."

Tuggy looked at Monica and walked out of the door.

**

Tuggy pulled up at A-Dog's trap. He jumped out of the car, gun in hand and ran inside. "Yo, A-Dog, this nigga Pillz just tripped all the way the fuck out homie."

A-Dog jumped up. "What the fuck happened bro? Where this nigga at?"

"I don't know where the fuck boy is at. Him and some niggas was up in my spot when Monica came home. They roughed her up, put a gun to her dome and told her they will body her just to deliver a message to me. They got my bitch at home scared as fuck. Then, they told her they will kill her family."

"That nigga really went against the grain, bringing family in this shit."

Tuggy sat down at the table shaking his head as his knee bounced in jittery anger. "This nigga got to die bro. I ain't trying to hear shit else. That nigga want it to be up, then it's guns up."

"Come on then. Let's ride out then. Niggas like him ain't hard to find. Just blaze on sight."

"You already know."

**

"Pillz, what's the move?"

"To put these niggas in the dirt."

"You think Tuggy got that message?"

"Fucking right he did, Buckshot. I'll send a lot more his way too."

Pillz looked at the group of niggas he had on the block selling his shit. Not only was he moving weight, but he was also the ruler like Mo'nay told him he could be. His presence was known to everybody.

**

"You see what I see, Tuggy?" Tuggy looked to the left and saw Pillz in the park with a group of people talking.

"You, ready to let loose?"

"Yeah, let's do this, A-Dog."

Pillz looked at the black Honda pulling up to the park. As the windows rolled down. "Oh shit, down, down. Drive by."

A-Dog stuck his arm out of the window and shot a .45 into the crowd of people. Tuggy jumped out the car shooting a Mac-11. All you saw was people running for cover. Pillz pulled his gun out and started shooting from behind a tree in the park.

"Yeah, motherfucker, I got your message and I'm here to answer your call in person."

"Good motherfucker, ring ring."

Pillz jumped from behind the tree, shooting his .357 at Tuggy. The car windows shattered as Tuggy jumped back into the car with A-Dog and took off. Pillz looked at the car peeling off. He ran into the street and started shooting at the car. He turned and saw two of his souljas on the ground covered in blood. You could hear the police sirens in the distance coming their way. "Pillz look, get up out of here. I got this bro." Pillz dapped Buckshot up before running to his car and driving off. As he cut the corner and sped away from the park, the police shot past him and towards the commotion.

**

"That's how you handle business, Tuggy, hands down. We pull up. We don't do no talking and we let the fuck off. You saw them bodies drop when that hot lead hit they ass, nigga?"

"Word, I was trying to dome check, Pillz. I wanted that nigga soul snatched from his body."

"We just laid two of his boys out. I saw when they hit the ground. They last words had better been a prayer to God to ask forgiveness for their sins."

"Fuck them niggas. Just be ready because we know Pillz is coming back at us. We need to be on point when he do."

"You know what, Tuggy? We need to move from Miller Ave. before Pillz try something. He knows that's one of our stash spots."

"When you trying to do that?"

"Sometime this week. We can when shit cool down a little."

"Say less, we need to dump this car somewhere before we get pulled over in it."

"We doing that right now."

SAYNOMORE

Chapter Thirty-Two

Pillz sat at the table quietly thinking when his phone went off. He looked and saw it was Buckshot calling him. "Yo, what's the word?"

"Ace is dead but Double R is good. He got hit in the shoulder."

"Damn, okay. Good looking out for letting me know. Let me try and put the pieces together for this puzzle because shit went all wrong today."

"Hit me up when it's time to put that work in."

"Already."

Pillz hung up the phone as Mo'nay came walking down the stairs. She ran her finger across Pillz shoulder and sat down at the table on the side of him. "What went wrong today?"

"One of my guys got shot and the other one killed."

Mo'nay took her hand and grabbed Pillz hand and looked into his eyes. "I'm sorry about your soulja but Tuggy and A-Dog know how you move already. To beat them you have to move differently. You have to move like Dope Boy, not Pillz."

"Yeah, I know. I'm thinking on how to do that now."

"Think about this. Pillz has love for them, Dope Boy don't. They know what Pillz is going to do, but they don't know what Dope Boy is going to do. Remember I, just wanted to see you win, Anthony. From the very beginning, and now look where we are. Have I told you anything wrong yet?"

"No, you haven't."

"And I'm not. I promise you that."

Pillz kissed Mo'nay's hand. "I know you got my back."

"So, trust me. War costs money. Hit them where it hurts. Do you know where they keep their work at?"

"Yeah, I do. If they ain't changed spots."

"Good. We are not going to take it. Set the spot on fire to show them we are not thieves but we ain't fucked up either."

"When?"

"Tonight."

Mo'nay got up and kissed Pillz forehead before going upstairs.

**

It was late. Pillz had on a black hoodie and black sweatpants. He was in the bushes across the street from the stash house. He looked both ways down Miller Ave. to make sure nobody was on the block. Then, he ran across the street to the back of the house. He took out a pocket knife and popped the backdoor open. He poured gas all over the house, up the stairs and in every room. He walked into the living room and saw the five brown flags hanging on the living room wall.

As much as he hated Tuggy and A-Dog, these flags represented Browns and he wouldn't disrespect the set. He took his flag, Tuggy's A-Dog's, Murder's, and Trap's flag down. He put his flag in his pocket. He looked around one more time and dropped a match. He walked out the backdoor as the house went up in flames. He placed the other four flags in the mailbox as he left the block.

Once in his car, he looked back and saw the flames going through the roof of the house.

Chapter Thirty-Three

"A-Dog, how much was in the house?"

"Everything, but the money."

"How much money we got put up?"

"Like two hundred and twenty thousand. Plus, I've got ten bricks at my spot."

"We had over thirty kilos in that spot that went up in flames and we still owe the plug."

"Look, Manny know we don't play games and we never came up short before. We can stretch all ten bricks into fifteen and we are good."

"Yeah, word came to me today that only one of them niggas got killed too."

"Shit, well, we up and that's all that matters. We got a body under our belt and we still on our feet. We took a big ass loss today, but that shit is going to come back. That nigga Pillz know he got a death wish tatted on his back. He better stay bullet proofed up because them shells is coming."

"Yeah, let's go get that work. We got to hug the block homie."

**

Three days later.

Mo'nay sat in the car looking at Monica as she walked into her house. She pulled the black BMW up in front. She got out of the car and knocked on the door two times.

"Who is it?"

"Mo'nay."

When Monica opened the door, she looked at Mo'nay. "And who are you?"

"The bitch that A-Dog shot." Mo'nay looked at Monica as she turned to run back into the house. Mo'nay grabbed her by the hair and pulled her down. She pulled out her knife and slit Monica's throat from ear to ear. She took two steps back as she watched the blood come out of her throat. Monica looked up at Mo'nay as she grabbed her throat with the blood pouring out. Her eyes were rolling to the back of her head. Mo'nay walked to the table, picked up Monica's phone, and texted Tuggy.

Hey, bae, can you come by the house? I need to talk with you, kisses.

She put the phone down on the table, walked back out of the house to her car and drove off. She knew what she would have to do to prove her point. She was not to be fucked with.

**

"How we looking over there, Tuggy?"

"Beautiful, we almost at that five K mark." A-Dog was smoking a blunt and bagging up the last few grams he had broken down. "Yeah, nigga we can't be stopped. Word got back to me where Pillz be holding his weight in the Dance. We need to pay that spot a visit."

"How the hell you find that out?"

"I gave up a quarter of a bird for the information. I was going to let that shit ride, but I hope he's in there when we roll up."

Tuggy looked at his phone as it went off. "Yo, my baby girl Monica just hit me up. I knew she couldn't be mad at me for long. She asking me to pull up. You got the rest of his shit, bro?"

"Yeah, lover boy. I got it. Go handle your business."

Tuggy put his phone in his pocket, gave A-Dog a pound and walked outside to his car. He texted Monica back.

I'm on my way now, bae.

**

Tuggy walked into the house and stopped in his tracks. In a state of shock, he put his back against the wall and slid down to the floor as he wiped the tears out of his eyes. He placed his gun on the floor next to him as he looked at his wifey. The lady who was carrying his unborn child was laying on the floor dead with her throat cut from ear to ear. "No, Monic, no. Fuck, baby, I should have been here. I'm sorry, baby girl. I'm so sorry." Tuggy got up and moved everything in the house from drugs, guns, and money. He picked up his phone and called A-Dog. After a few rings, A-Dog picked up. "Yo-Yo what's good, lover boy?"

Tuggy was crying as he talked on the phone. "She dead, bro. Them niggas killed my wifey and my unborn child. They took her away from me, bro."

"Tuggy, you telling me Monica is dead?"

"Yeah, they cut her throat from ear to ear. I walked in the house, and she was lying in a pool of blood on the floor."

"But she just texted you."

"It wasn't her. Whoever did this wanted me to find her body first. They texted me from her phone and put it on the table and left. Fuck, homie. Fuck!"

"Damn, Tuggy, fuck bro. I'm sorry, fam." A-Dog just listened as Tuggy cried over his baby mother. He never heard his homie this way before and knew Pillz had crossed the ultimate line now.

Chapter Thirty-Four

"Buckshot, tell me something good. How we looking out here?"

"We on point and catching plays. We ain't trying to get caught down bad again. Other than that, we good."

"Yeah, be on point. We fucked them over the last few nights. We took their legs right out from under them."

"Yeah, I heard how Tuggy came home and his bitch throat was cut from ear to ear. She was carrying his baby."

Pillz looked at Buckshot when he said that in a state of confusion. "Say that shit again."

"Yeah, that nigga Tuggy's baby mom got rolled and she was carrying his child."

"When this shit happen?"

"Like two days ago. I thought you knew about it."

"Y'all stay posted up on the block. I got some shit I need to deal with." Pillz dapped Buckshot up and walked off. He pulled his phone out and called Mo'nay. She picked it up after a few rings.

"Hello?"

"Hey, where you at?"

"On my way back to the house. Why what's up?"

"We need to talk. I'm on my way to your spot now."

"Okay, I'll be there in twenty minutes."

"I'll see you in a minute then." Pillz hung up the phone and headed to Mo'nay's house. He knew she played a part in Monica's murder. He just had to hear it out of her mouth and why she did what she did.

**

"A-Dog, it's good to see you again. Like always, I know the count is correct."

"It's good to see you as well, Manny and yes it's five K on the head."

"Is there something you want to ask me? I see the expression on your face."

"Yes, it's about Mo'nay. Do you know who she is?"

Manny looked at A-Dog, got up from his desk and closed the office door. "Why you ask me about her? And why do you even know about her?

"I met her through Omar over six years ago."

"Mo'nay, Mo'nay. Omar kept the little bitch around up here where nobody would know?"

"What's up with her, Manny?"

"Mo'nay was bought at the age of nine or ten. Omar showed her all the wrong ways as a child. Mo'nay is a very good manipulator. She knows how to turn family and friends against each other, and she is very patient. A big part of that is because Omar made her do things a child should have never been doing. She is not to be trusted at all."

"I think she had my homie's baby mother killed, not to speak on all the other shit she did five years ago that I'm just finding out about now."

"A bitch like Mo'nay is better off dead than alive. She will cut your throat and watch you bleed, trust me. I can tell you stories about Mo'nay and the shit she did. It's because of her Omar was in the position he was in. She was whatever he needed her to be; a whore, lover, or priest. He was the only one who could control her. She plays dirty tricks and don't respect the rules. Everything is fair to her."

"So, why y'all never killed her?"

"Because she was his child. Blood don't make you related. Loyalty do and she was devoted to him."

"What if she had him killed, then what?"

"We all know she did, but he made his bed and it cost him his life."

A-Dog got up and shook Manny's hand before leaving.

"A-Dog to kill a fox you have to set a trap, but first you must lure it out of its den or the trap is useless."

A-Dog nodded as he walked out of the door.

**

Mo'nay opened the front door for Pillz to come inside. He stepped up and kissed her on the check before walking into the house. Mo'nay closed the door and walked behind Pillz to the dining room table.

"What's that expression on your face, Anthony?"

"Did you have Tuggy's baby mother killed?"

"No, I didn't have her killed. I killed the bitch myself, why?"

"She was carrying his child, Mo'nay."

"Pillz, I got shot and you could have been killed. We left them niggas alone for over a year and let them have Amityville. You gave them a bottle of Cîroc to show there was no hard feelings and the first thing they do is shoot at us. So, I don't have no feelings for them. That bitch and her baby is in a better place now.. or not."

"I thought you said you was going to let me handle it, Mo'nay."

"I am and you are."

Mo'nay got up and placed her hands on Pillz' shoulders and started to rub them. She could tell he was upset and very tense. She leaned over and kissed his ear. "This is your boat, Anthony and I'll let you steer it."

After she said that, she took her tongue and licked his neck. Pillz closed his eyes and leaned his head back. She took her hand, unbuttoned his pants, grabbed his manhood and pulled it out. She played with it until it was brick hard. Pillz still had his eyes closed, loving the moment. Mo'nay made her way to the front of Pillz and climbed on top of him. She let her warm, wet box slide down his thick pole. Pillz opened his mouth and let out a moan at the sensation of how tight she was. Mo'nay rode Pillz nice and slow as she kissed all over him, going up and down on his manhood. Pillz couldn't hold it back no longer as he listened to Mo'nay's moans and the feeling of her hot box and body on his. He felt her juices going down his pole and Pillz grabbed Mo'nay as he released all his seeds inside of her. Mo'nay looked at Pillz as he opened his eyes. She kissed him on the forehead and got up.

"I'm sorry for going behind your back, Anthony. It won't happen again." Mo'nay looked at Pillz, who was still lost in the blissful spell she just put on him.

For many days after, he thought of having sex with Mo'nay and the way she sexed him down like that had him stuck in his own world. To Pillz, it was amazing but to Mo'nay, she just did what she had to do to keep Pillz under her control. He was too big an investment for her to lose and if fucking him was going to be the key that held it all together, then his car was going to stay parked in her garage.

Chapter Thirty-Five

A-Dog looked at Tuggy in his all black suit as he stood over Monica's casket with a red rose in his hands. "How you holding up, bro?"

"I'm burying the lady who was carrying my child today, A-Dog. Her and my unborn child is dead over my bullshit. They both was innocent and now they dead. I told you to leave that shit alone. That the nigga, Pillz and his bitch wasn't fucking with us. Now, we lost kilos, my family is dead and you going to ask me how am I holding up?"

"We going to get this bitch and kill her ass; you have my word."

"Killing her won't bring Monica or my child back. After this last run A-Dog, I'm done. You can have it all." Tuggy looked at A-Dog and placed the rose on the casket and walked away.

**

Pillz looked at his phone as it went off with a text message. He picked his phone up and saw the message didn't have a name, just a number.

Pillz we need to talk can you meet me under the bridge tonight at eight P.M. Just me and you. No funny business, on Browns.

"Pillz placed his phone on the table and walked into the kitchen where Mo'nay was at. "What you making to eat?"

"Something light, nothing too heavy. Why?"

"I wouldn't mind a bite to eat." Pillz loved the way Mo'nay's style made her a sexy, boss bitch that knew how to treat a nigga right. It was because of her he was winning. In all his years, he never felt a love like this before and he didn't want to lose it.

"Then you need to go to the bathroom and wash your hands. I'll set the table up for us."

"Are you telling me or asking me?"

"I'm telling you."

Pillz kissed Mo'nay on the forehead and went to wash his hands in the bathroom. Mo'nay brought the food to the table. She moved Pillz phone to the side and his screen came on. She looked at the message on the screen and read it. Then, she cut the screen off and went to get the rest of the food off the stove.

"You need some help with that?"

"No, I got it. Here I come now."

Pillz picked up his phone and put it in his pocket as he sat at the kitchen table. "Mo'nay, this smells and looks good as hell."

"Of course it does, nigga. I made it."

"There you go. I should have never gave you the big head."

"Whatever, so what's your plans for tonight?"

"I have to make a big drop off with Buckshot around seven. Then, I'm going to meet that nigga A-Dog under the bridge tonight around eight. He got my new number from someone and hit me up. He said no funny business, but I never replied back to his text."

"You need to find out how he got your number. That's dangerous. Are you going to text him back?"

"I don't know. A part of me wants to hear what he's got to say, another part of me don't give a fuck about what he has to say."

Mo'nay looked at Pillz, got up and walked to the kitchen.

"Mo'nay, I see that look on your face. What's on your mind, baby girl?"

"Nothing at all."

"Mo'nay, don't be like that."

"Anthony, I told you I was going to let you drive this boat and I meant that."

"I understand that but what's wrong?"

Mo'nay looked at Pillz. "Going to meet him is a sign of weakness on your part. Let him meet you on your terms and your time when you're ready to meet him."

"So do I reply back?"

"No, you have his number now. You reply back when you're ready and not today."

"You really are a boss bitch. So…what are we exactly?"

"Pillz, baby, we don't need a title to know what we are."

Pillz pulled Mo'nay close to him and hugged her tight.

**

A-Dog sat under the bridge for over an hour, waiting on Pillz to show up. He looked at his watch and saw it was nine P.M. He got in his car and drove off. It took him twenty minutes to get back to the trap. He stepped out of the car and went inside. Mo'nay sat at the top of the corner and watched him in her Lexus.

A-Dog was so lost in his thoughts about talking with Pillz he didn't see the Lexus follow him from the bridge. He just knew he had to end this between the two of them, no matter the risk. Mo'nay sat at the corner for the next hour before she pulled off. A-Dog was her enemy as well as Tuggy, and if Pillz wasn't going to kill them, she would go another way to do it. She was still going to have her cake and eat it too.

SAYNOMORE

Chapter Thirty-Six

"Tuggy, you need to put the bottle down while you're cooking that dope up. We can't afford no losses."

"I been doing this shit forever. I got this. Just do you over there."

"You know what? I'm about to make two drops. I'll leave you to what the fuck you doing, homie."

"Yeah, do that. I'm straight over here."

A-Dog looked at Tuggy as he walked out the door, knowing he wasn't in his right mind.

**

Tuggy looked out the window as A-Dog car drove off. All he saw was the back of A-Dog's head lights leaving the block. He was packing up all of the work in plastic bags when he heard a knock at the door.

"Who is it?"

He went to open the door and two men dressed in black rushed him. Tuggy's gun fell off his hip and slid under the couch. He went to grab it and was knocked down and kicked in the face. He fell on his back in a state of dizziness as he was kicked and punched over and over again. He grabbed one of the attackers and pulled him down to the floor. Then, he jumped up and tackled the other guy to the floor and kicked him in the face. He grabbed a crowbar one of his attackers dropped and smacked the other guy in the back of the head, knocking him out cold. Then, he ran up to the other guy and smacked him in the face. Tuggy threw the crow bar down, walked to the couch and picked up his gun from underneath it.

"Ya motherfuckers thought I was a free pack, running up in my shit. You pussy ass fuck boys." Tuggy stomped one of them over and over in the stomach. "Who the fuck sent you to die?" Tuggy walked up to one of the men and pulled his mask off. He looked into unfamiliar eyes. "Who the fuck are you?" Tuggy looked at the man lying next to the unknown attacker. He walked over and snatched his mask off in a rage. Tuggy put the gun to the guy's head and pulled the trigger, blowing his brains out on the floor. He looked at the other guy. "Whoever sent you, got you killed nigga." Tuggy pulled the trigger two times, bullets slammed into the man's face and blood splattered all over the room. Tuggy walked to the front door and looked out of it. He couldn't believe someone tried to rob him and have him killed.

**

"Pillz, what's the word on the block."

"Nigga you know I don't be on no fucking block. I'm just sitting in the park smoking a blunt. Buckshot, you going to make me put some buckshots in your ass."

"You know I'm just fucking with you. You look like you stressing though for real."

"No, I just got a lot on my mind and some shit I'm trying to figure out."

"Look, I know what you need."

"And what's that?"

Pillz looked at Buckshot as they sat in the park smoking.

"Some pussy. Them two twins, Crystal and Diamond are at the spot right now. I know you don't want to pass that up."

"Bro, I been fucking Mo'nay for the last few days. We ain't got no title or nothing but I don't know how to take it."

"If you fucking Mo'nay homie, you winning!"

"Yeah, everything I got is the shit. I'm flooding the blocks with dope because of her."

"Look, big homie, niggas wasn't fucking with the Dance until you came out here showing love. Just know we got your back and move on your call."

Pillz dapped Buckshot up. "So, can I smoke that blunt with you?"

"Hell naw. I don't know where your lips have been."

Pillz punched Buckshot in the arm, then passed him the blunt. "I'm about to head to the spot. I'll link up with you tomorrow."

"Cool, tell Mo'nay I said what's up."

"Copy that, bro."

**

A-Dog walked into the trap and saw two dead bodies on the floor and Tuggy at the table drinking out a bottle of Cîroc.

"What the fuck happened in here?"

"Somebody tried to kill me, A-Dog, but they fucked it up and got themselves killed.

"How long ago this happen?"

"Not even ten minutes after you left." Tuggy got up and walked to one of the bodies on the floor and showed A-Dog what was left of his face. "You know this nigga?"

"He don't have a fucking face, Tuggy. Look, we need to get that shit the fuck up out of here and burn this bitch down before we get charged with two bodies."

"Man, fuck that shit. I'm waiting on the motherfucker who sent them to send some more niggas for me to body."

"Tuggy, you are drunk right now and you ain't in your right mind."

"I'm good, remember? Bang bang. Fuck them and the police."

"Look, where is the work at?"

"Over there in the cabinets where it's always at."

A-Dog went and gathered all the dope and put it in a bookbag. Then, placed it in the car. He went back inside the trap. Tuggy was so drunk he wasn't thinking right. A-Dog walked behind him and smacked him in the head with his gun, knocking him out cold. He picked his body up, took him to the car and closed the door. He got Tuggy's car keys and drove off on the side of Friendly Barbershop. He ran back down the block to check the trap and make sure he wasn't leaving nothing inside. He turned on all the eyes on the stove, set the couch on fire and ran out of the house to his car and drove off. By the time he hit the corner, the house was in full flames.

**

Mo'nay watched the video camera from the apartment. She had in the basement. As she cooked up some kilos in the apartment, she watched Pillz pull up to the house. She heard the front door open.

"Mo'nay, where you at?"

"I'm in the basement, Anthony."

Pillz placed the keys on the table and walked down stairs to the basement. He walked up to Mo'nay and gave her a kiss on the lips. "I see what you been doing down here."

"Yeah, just stretching some kilos out. They were ninety seven percent pure, so I broke ten of them down and made fifteen. So, they're about eighty-eight percent now."

Pillz couldn't take his eyes off Mo'nay as she stood down there with her hair pulled back, wearing nothing but a G-string, apron, and ankle socks. "Damn, you look sexy as hell right now, bae."

"I do?"

"Yes, you do. My little Betty Crocker."

"Well, wrap this last kilo up for me while I clean up these glass pots. Then, you can come upstairs with me and tell me what happened today out there while we take a bath together."

"That sounds just like a plan. We can definitely make that move, Mo'nay."

Mo'nay smiled as she walked to the kitchen sink.

Chapter Thirty-Seven

It was two P.M. when Tuggy woke up on the couch. His body was stiff, and he had a knot in the back of his head.

"Damn, where the fuck am I? Why my body feel so stiff like this?"

"You at my spot, Tuggy. You don't remember what happened last night?"

"Shit is blurry to me."

"You peter rolled two niggas last night. They kicked in the door and tried to clap you, but you put they ass to bed. Check this out."

A-Dog cut the T.V. on and put it on the news so Tuggy could see and hear what happened last night. "Yeah, I told you to put that bottle down. You was white boy wasted last night but I got all the work out the spot, moved your car then put the trap in flames because our fingerprints was on everything in that bitch."

"So, motherfuckers thought we was a lick?"

"Yeah, they did. It had to be some new jack ass niggas because they had a crowbar and bat, no guns. I don't know what the fuck they was thinking."

"You think this was Mo'nay and Pillz shit?"

"No, them niggas ain't have guns. They was just some niggas who was broke and trying to come up."

"You ain't got no pain pills in this bitch? My head is banging right now."

"Yeah, let me go get you some."

Tuggy leaned back on the couch and closed his eyes as A-Dog went and got him some pain pills. Tuggy still couldn't believe what happened last night. Shit was getting too real in the hood when niggas thought he was a lick.

**

A-Dog's phone went off. He looked and saw it was Pillz that texted him.

"Meet me under the train tracks in one hour. On Browns, no funny business. I just want talk."

A-Dog replied back. "I'll be there."

"Tuggy, this nigga Pillz just him me up. He's trying to talk. He wants to meet up in an hour under the train tracks. I told him I'll be there."

"I'm riding with you."

"What you think he want to talk about?"

"We'll see when we get there."

Tuggy got up slow. His body was still stiff, and his head ached. He picked up his gun from off the table and put it on his waist. "Let's ride out. I want to be there when he pulls up."

"Facts, let's ride then."

**

Pillz sat at the table loading up his Glock-9 and making sure he had an extra clip. He looked at his watch and saw it was time to go. He walked outside and got into his Jeep 4 x 4 and headed towards the tracks. He just hoped A-Dog played it fair and wasn't on no slime shit. When he pulled up, he saw A-Dog and Tuggy both standing in the front of Pillz' car. He stopped a few feet in front of them and got out. He looked to see where both of their hands was at as he walked to the front of his Jeep. "Tuggy, A-Dog."

"What's up, Pillz? What's on your mind?"

Pillz looked at A-Dog when he said that. "I came here to see if we can dead this beef. We can't make money when we shooting at each other. Soon, the Feds is going to come in on this shit and we all are going to be behind bars before this is all over. Ain't nobody going to win. We all are going to suffer in the end."

"Nigga you killed my wife and unborn child. This ain't about fucking winning. Nigga you took it to a new level. I don't care about a casket or a prison cell. Shit is to that point now."

"So, why you agree to the meeting then?"

"Because I wanted to look into the nigga eyes who I once called my brother one last time before I kill his ass."

A-Dog stepped in front of Tuggy. "Y'all niggas chill. Pillz you crossed the line in more ways than one: you set the trap on fire with thirty kilos inside, you killed the homie's wife and unborn child, and I don't know if it was you or not that sent someone to kill Tuggy last night. Right now, all fingers are pointing towards you."

"Y'all started this shit. Y'all drew first blood. I bounced with no hard feelings, gave you niggas a bottle and all. The first thing you niggas do is try and catch me down bad in a parking lot as I'm leaving."

A-Dog looked at Tuggy and at Pillz. "Pillz, you think that bitch got love for you? She using you nigga. You can't see that?"

"You know what I see? Some envious ass niggas. I'm up right now. When I was trying to build with you, you would drop me one or two kilos off. Everything was between you and that nigga. Now I'm the plug, supplying motherfuckers twenty and thirty kilos at a time. So, how the fuck is she using me nigga? Look A-Dog, I ain't come here to see whose dick is bigger. I come here to see if we can end this shit for good."

Tuggy looked at Pillz. "Yeah, we can do that, Pillz."

Pillz looked at A-Dog then pulled his gun out as Tuggy started shooting at him. Pillz was running backwards, shooting his gun at both of them. "You said on Browns, A-Dog. That shit don't mean nothing no more?"

"The only way to make this right is with your body lying in a pool of blood, Pillz. There is no going back to the way it was and this shit can't end with no peace talk."

Pillz looked at his Jeep and where A-Dog and Tuggy both were ducked behind the car. "Fuck it, let's all go out with a real bang then, niggas." Pillz ran out from behind the pole, shooting at the car. He jumped in his Jeep and took off backwards. A-Dog and Tuggy came from behind their car and started to shoot at his Jeep as he backed up. Pillz turned the Jeep around and floored it out of there. "Fuck. You think you hit him, A-Dog?"

"I don't know, I saw him grab his arm though."

"Fuck, come on. Let's get up out of here before the boys come."

Pillz was looking at the holes in his windshield as he was driving back to his spot. His right shoulder was bleeding because he got shot in it. He pulled over to see how bad it was, but it was just a bad graze. When he pulled up to his spot, he closed his eyes and sat in the Jeep for a minute before going inside.

**

Mo'nay pulled up in the driveway and saw the holes in Pillz' Jeep windshield and door. She walked into the house and saw drops of blood on the floor, going up the stairs to the bathroom. She pulled her gun out and walked up the stairs to the bathroom. She saw Pillz standing in front of the mirror with his gun on the sink, cleaning his wound out. Blood was dripping down his arm into the sink.

"Anthony, what happened to you?"

"It's a long story."

Mo'nay walked to the bathroom closet got some more towels to help clean Pillz' gunshot wound. "Let me see how bad it is. Move your hand."

Pillz moved his hand and Mo'nay looked at his shoulder. "It's not that bad. Now, tell me what happened while I patch this up."

"Long story short, me, Tuggy and A-Dog got into a shootout today."

"Where at?"

"Amityville, under the train tracks."

"Why were you in Amityville under the train tracks?"

"I went to meet with them to see if we can end this beef with each other."

"Wait, you went to meet with them by yourself? How dumb was that Anthony? They don't give a fuck about you."

"Mo'nay, A-Dog put it on Browns."

"I don't give a fuck if he put it on the blood of Jesus. Look what the fuck happened. You got shot, blood is all over the fucking house and bullet holes are in the Jeep outside because he put it on a fucking color."

"Mo'nay."

"Anthony, I don't want to talk. Your shoulder is bandaged up and now I have blood to clean up."

Pillz watched as Mo'nay walked out the bathroom, slamming the door behind her.

Chapter Thirty-Eight

"Mo'nay is the one who killed Monica, Tuggy. I saw it in Pillz eyes yesterday. He had the chance to kill her before and he didn't. He really was trying to end this shit."

"A-Dog, I don't give a fuck what he was trying to do. The point is my wife and unborn child is dead. That nigga ain't shit to me and if he ain't do it, his fucking bitch did. So, he got just as much blood on his hands as she do. I got shells for both of them."

"Well shit, I know he got that message last night when that hot lead his ass."

"I hope that nigga crashed and he somewhere on the side of the road bleeding to death."

A-Dog ain't say nothing. He just sat at the table rolling up a blunt and watching Tuggy pace the floor.

**

Pillz sat in the basement listening to Mo'nay play *Sure Thing* by Miguel and smoking a blunt. He thought back to how A-Dog set him up to get killed, knowing Mo'nay was right. They was brothers in the past and enemies of today. Pillz looked as Mo'nay walked downstairs, She walked up to him and sat next to him on the couch. "You still upset at me?"

"Yes, I am. You could have got yourself killed trusting an old friendship. What you had ain't the same. You're on a level they are trying to reach and there's been too much blood on the streets spilled to go back to how you used to be."

"I know it was stupid. I just thought they would play it fair on the up and up."

Mo'nay took the blunt out of Pillz' hand and put it in the ashtray. She held his hands in hers as she looked into his eyes.

"Anthony, it's time both of them die before it's too late and you end up dead."

"They are going to be on point and waiting for me to strike. I know they are."

"I let you drive the boat and you crashed. It's my turn to take the wheel now."

"Mo'nay."

"No."

"Okay, then, Let me do this, baby."

"I trust you, bae."

Mo'nay kissed Pillz on the lips, then started to sing Miguel's song Sure Thing. Mo'nay was everything to Pillz and she knew that. "I'll be back, Anthony. Stay here and relax." Mo'nay kissed him one more time before walking off.

**

Mo'nay pulled up to Wild Bill's, a bar where cops hung out at. She stepped out of her black BMW and walked inside. She looked around and made eye contact with who she needed to see. She took a seat at the end table on the back wall. She watched as the officer approached her.

"Mo'nay, it's been a while. How have you been?"

"Good, trying to be a ghost, Dererick."

"So, tell me, what brings this ghost out of her grave?"

Mo'nay looked around to make sure no one was watching her. She slid an envelope across the table to Dererick. "That's ten thousand dollars. I need a body, bring to me."

Dererick looked inside the envelope and placed it in his jacket pocket. "Who's the body and where can I find him at?"

"You can find him on Albany Avenue or Smith Street area."

"So, he's one of them Browns boys?"

"I guess, I don't know."

"You still ain't give me a name."

Mo'nay looked at Dererick. "Tuggy."

"I know who he is. Where you want me to bring him to?"

"We haven't been to the beach in a while, have we?"

"No, we haven't. Same dock?"

"Yes."

"You have the same number?"

"Sure do, it never changes."

Dererick smiled as he got up from the table and walked away. Mo'nay followed behind him a few seconds later.

**

"A-Dog, what we doing here tonight?"

"Look, Tuggy, we been beefing and doing all the fuck shit. I'm trying to forget about the last two weeks. We got a poker table over there I'm trying to sit at. There's a dice table over there, a bar with the games on above it and a backroom where you can get some good wet wet. Nigga, what I'm trying to say is, let's enjoy the night."

"Yeah, fuck it. I'll be at the bar if you need me."

"I'm over here at the tables. I'm about to break them bitches."

"What's the word, A-Dog. Where the hell you been?"

"You don't need to worry about that. You got some money for me to take from you tonight?"

"I see you come back with jokes. What you want, dice or cards?"

"You know what, Little Lee, because it's you, I'll take whatever you got left on them dice.

"You talking big money shit, A-Dog. I'll make sure you walk out of here broke."

"Damn, you talking all that shit, Little Lee. You ain't rolled the dice yet."

"A-Dog say less. Yo, baby girl, let me get two bottles of Grey Goose over here."

"About time, now roll the dice." A-Dog was talking shit, rolling dice, smoking weed and taking shots while Tuggy was at the bar watching the games drinking Cîroc Jell-O shots and smoking. Tuggy got up and stumbled to the dice table. "Yo, A-Dog, I'm going outside to get some fresh air."

"Hold up, I'm coming with you."

Tuggy and A-Dog walked outside smoking a cigarette and standing by the backdoor to the bar. "Yo, A-Dog, real shit, I'm white boy wasted."

"You too?" Little Lee done popped me for fifteen Gs fucking with them dice."

"Damn, and all that shit you was talking when you first walked in the spot."

"Look, I'm going back in there as soon as I finish my smoke."

"Cool, I'm at the tables."

Tuggy watched as A-Dog went inside. He leaned against the wall as his phone went off. He looked at the screen but didn't recognize the number. "Yo, who is this?"

"D-Nice, man."

"Oh okay, what's up?"

"I was trying to cop some work from you."

"Shit bro, I only have two grams on me right now."

"That's cool. Where you at?"

"I'm on Dickerson Avenue at the Dugout Bar and Grill. How long before you pull up?"

"Ten minutes, I'm on my way now."

"I'll be on the main road out front."

"I'll pull over when I see you."

Tuggy hung up the phone and walked up the stairs from the Dugout and stood on the main road.

D-nice looked at the cop with the gun on him.

"Now, you better not say shit, D-nice, because you are the number one suspect in that double homicide in that house fire three weeks ago off Albany Ave. You know, where the two dope heads were beat, shot in the face and set on fire. There's no beating that in court. Walk down the road and forget we ever had this conversation. Now, get on before I change my mind and lock your ass up on everything."

D-nice looked at Dererick and walked off.

Tuggy was standing on Dickerson Ave when the black van pulled up. He walked to the sliding doors. When the door opened, he tensed. His body locked up as he hit the ground. Dererick jumped out and cuffed Tuggy up and threw him in the van. He jumped in and drove off. Then, he picked up his phone and called Mo'nay. Mo'nay rolled over in her bed and looked at the time. It was eleven forty-five p.m. She picked up her ringing phone.

"Hello."

"I'm going to have a swim; you might want to come."

Mo'nay sat up in bed. "I'm on my way now."

"Last dock, tied up like always."

"Okay."

Mo'nay hung up the phone and went to get up. "Baby, where you going?"

"I have to go take care of something."

"This late at night?"

"Yeah."

Pillz looked at Mo'nay. "I'm coming with you."

"Anthony, are you sure you want to come with me? I'm driving the boat now and I don't have mixed feelings when it comes to doing what it takes to win."

"Mo'nay, I said I'm coming, baby girl."

Mo'nay looked at Pillz and nodded. "Come on then. I can't keep him waiting."

Mo'nay and Pillz pulled up in the night fog at Tainn Park at twelve twenty A.M. Dererick saw the blue headlights from the BMW pulling up. He backed out of the parking space and pulled off when Mo'nay pulled up. He flashed his lights twice at her as he drove off.

Pillz looked at the van as it drove off. "Who was that?"

"A friend. Come on, we have a gift at the end of the pier waiting for us."

Mo'nay opened up her glove box, pulled her .9 mm pistol out and put it in her pocket. She opened the car door. "Come on, Anthony."

Pillz just looked around at the heavy fog covering the surface of the water and pier. Mo'nay walked to the end of the pier and stopped as she looked at Tuggy tied to the pole of the pier. Pillz looked at Tuggy, then Mo'nay.

"Tuggy is it?"

"Bitch if I wasn't tied up, I would kill your fucking ass. You think I'm fucking scared?"

"No, I know you're not scared, Mr. Big Bad Wolf but you do know the wolf died at the end of the story."

Tuggy looked at Pillz. "Nigga, you standing here with her? We go back to the fucking sandbox."

Pillz ain't say nothing.

Mo'nay looked at Pillz, then back at Tuggy. "Tuggy I killed Monica. I cut her throat from the back. Anthony ain't even know I did it. She tried to run but I grabbed her and after I cut her throat, I watched her bleed out. Then, I texted you from her phone so you would find her body lying there, dead in a pool of blood."

"You think this shit is going to end with me? A-Dog ain't going to let this ride. Pillz you soft as fuck. You ain't no bossed up nigga. You are a puppet and she just stringing you along. Moving you the way she want you too."

"Tuggy, you are boring me." Mo'nay walked up to Tuggy, pulled her gun out and put it on the side of his head. She looked at Pillz and put the gun up. She walked over to him and kissed him on the lips as she looked in his eyes. "How you want him to die, baby? Tell me."

Pillz just looked at Tuggy, then Mo'nay.

"Don't worry, Anthony. I got this, my king." Mo'nay walked up to Tuggy, pulled her knife out, slit his throat from ear to ear and walked off. "Come on baby, we have to go."

Pillz looked at the dead body one more time before walking off.

Chapter Thirty-Nine

A-Dog called Tuggy numerous times after he left the Dugout last night. He sat on the couch watching the news about the body found at Tanne Park beach pier with its throat cut from ear to ear. "Damn, niggas getting bodied everywhere in Amityville." A-Dog got up walked to the kitchen and put a bagel with butter in the microwave when his phone went off. He looked to see it was Kimberly calling him. He answered the phone. "Hello."

"Adem, did you see the news?"

"Yeah, I was just watching it. Niggas getting bodied left and right."

"You do know who that was, right?"

"No, they ain't say no name when I was watching it."

"Adem, that was Tuggy they found on the pier this morning."

"What the fuck?" A-Dog ran back in the living room to finish watching the news. When he saw Tuggy's picture on the screen, he couldn't believe what he was hearing. How was his body found, and his throat was cut from ear to ear, knowing he was just with him last night.

"Adem, Adem, you there?"

"Yo, Kim, let me call you back. This shit is crazy."

"Call me back, Adem."

"Yeah." A-Dog hung up the phone in a state of disbelief.

**

Mo'nay woke up and went to the bathroom. She washed her face and brushed her teeth like she normally did. She walked downstairs to the kitchen door and was looking at Pillz on the deck smoking a blunt. She walked to the sliding glass door and leaned against the door frame. "How long you been out here for?"

Pillz looked at Mo'nay. "About twenty minutes now."

"You still thinking about last night?"

"Yeah, I'm not going to lie to you. I am, Mo'nay."

"Anthony, that man tried to kill you. Look at all the bullet holes in your jeep. They shot you; he wanted you dead and I did what I had to do. A queen will protect her king, like the female lion will protect the male and her cubs. She will hunt for him, water the den and carry his cubs."

Pillz looked at Mo'nay as she walked up to him. She took his hand and placed it on her stomach.

'Mo'nay, are you?"

Mo'nay nodded. "Yes, I am. I'm three weeks now. I just found out the other day."

"I love you so fucking much."

"I love you too, but baby we have to finish what we started. A-Dog is playing Checkers while we play Chess. So we are going to win in the end, but I need you to stay focused with me."

"I'm here with you, baby girl. I swear I am." Pillz picked Mo'nay up and kissed her again. Over and over again.

"Good, now we can go eat."

"Yeah, let's eat, baby girl."

**

"This shit just don't make sense to me. I was just with Tuggy last night at the Dugout, Muncha."

"A-Dog, real shit. It's really on you. Not to be funny but when you beefing on the level you was beefing on, you don't never leave your nigga alone in the streets. Tuggy wasn't even in his right mind. He ain't been since baby girl got killed."

"That was my partner in crime for real, for real. This shit hurt like Murder all over again, Muncha." A-Dog sat on the stairs in the backyard smoking a blunt and talking with Muncha.

"A-Dog, I'll keep it all the way real with you. You're a shooter, and yeah, you know how to get your bread but you beefing with Pillz. Pillz is just a cool nigga who smoke weed and get money. The reason why he's up like that is because he's fucking with Don-Killer's bitch. Everybody who fuck with her eats. Nigga, you was side by side once upon a time. Let the streets tell the stories."

"I'll kill this nigga Pillz, on God. I don't care where I see this fool at or who he's with."

"Right now, what I'm about to say, don't take it the wrong way A-Dog, you need to just focus on getting your money up. Stop playing the blocks and sell weight so you know who is coming to see you."

"So, you saying let this shit ride?"

"No, I'm saying be smart. Get your money up first. Pillz did, and don't nobody know where he lives or what kind of car he's going to jump out of. Just being real with you."

"That is real talk, hands down, Muncha. I respect the jewels you dropping on me."

"Always. Look, I'm out. Stay up and here's my math if you need it." A-Dog took Muncha's number as he walked off, leaving A-Dog in the backyard smoking a blunt.

SAYNOMORE

Chapter Forty

"Mr. MIA, thirty days and running. Where the hell you been?

"Shit been crazy, Buckshot. I been making sure you got that work. How the paper looking?"

It's all right here. Twenty-one Gs homie. I really need another half."

"You know what, Buckshot? I was thinking about giving you a brick. You think you can work that one?"

"Hell yeah, what's the ticket on it?"

"On front, I want forty Gs. When you buy it COD, it's thirty-four. Is that good for you?"

"Yeah, I can do that. How long we talking?"

"Sixty days."

"Yeah, I can work that one."

"Let me get that paper off you real quick."

"Come inside the spot."

Pillz followed Buckshot inside the house and waited at the front door. Buckshot walked up to Pillz a few minutes later with a paper bag in his hand and handed it to him.

Pillz looked into the bag then nodded his head. "I like the way you do business."

"You fucking with me. I got to do you right."

"Copy that. Walk with me to my truck."

Pillz walked to his truck and sat inside. He pulled his blunt out of his ashtray and lit it. "Yo, I want you to be my number one man out here. I'll give you the key to these streets. Look at it like you going to be the new me out here. I'll supply you, and you are going to supply all of the niggas out here."

"I got your back. I ain't going to fuck it up."

"I know you're not. Pillz reached in the backseat of his truck and pulled out a bookbag. "Yo, there's a whole one in there. Hit me when you're ready to see me, homie. I'll pull up. But I'm about to ride out right now."

"Say less."

Buckshot dapped Pillz up and stepped out of the truck. He headed to the house as Pillz drove off.

**

A-Dog walked up to the dice game and watched the little homies talk shit and roll dice. He turned around when he heard someone call his name. "Yo, Willie, what's up, son?"

"Shit, niggas ain't seen you in a minute."

"Sometimes it's good not to be around. What's the word?"

"Same shit, different day."

"I see you got that boy D-Nice racking up all the money from these niggas."

"Man, I don't even fuck with that dude. He ain't living right."

"What you talking about?"

"I don't know the whole story, but word is he be talking to them jump out boys. You know, right there in the cut where he be trapping at, next to EZ Deli. I don't know which smoker it was, but they said they overheard him talking to Tuggy on the phone while the police had him against the wall. They took his .45 off him and everything. He was supposed to meet Tuggy on Dickerson Ave., but the police got in the van and left while D-Nice walked down the block.

Wait, hold on a fucking second. How long ago this was?"

"Right before he got killed."

"Man don't tell me that shit. Where at?"

"Smith Street, red house like always."

"Yo, I got to pull up on that shit. I'll pull back up."

"I'll be right here."

A-Dog walked off down the block to Smith Street. He looked and saw a few smokers standing next to the red house.

"Yo, yo, what's good with you?"

"A-Dog, let me find out you about to open up the candy shop. That's why you here?"

"Something like that. Yo, A.T., let me holla at you for a minute, baby girl?"

"Shit, here I come now, A-Dog. What's up?"

"Yo, word got back to me that some foul shit went down with D-Nice and the police. Tuggy's name was mixed up in that shit?"

"Look A-Dog, I just knew he called Tuggy for two grams and told the police everything that was said over the phone. He took D-Nice's gun and told him the two bodies and the house fire that went down over by the school was going to be pinned on him if he said a word. Then, he went to meet Tuggy on Dickerson Ave."

"Word, that's all the fuck I need to hear. You know the rat he was talking to?"

"You know the crooked motherfucker, Dererick?"

"Yeah, I know who you talking about." A-Dog reached in his pocket and pulled out a knot of hundreds. He peeled off three of them and handed them to A.T. "Good looking out for telling me that, ma."

"Shit, thank you."

A-Dog walked back to the dice game where D-Nice was still rolling dice and talking shit. Willie looked at A-Dog as he was walking up and began walking backwards from the crowd. A-Dog pulled out his .9 mm pistol and walked up to D-Nice while he was rolling dice. He pointed his gun at the back of D-Nice's head and pulled the trigger. D-Nice's body hit the ground. A-Dog ain't stop pulling the trigger until his clip was empty. He looked around at everyone and walked off, leaving D-Nice's blood all over the money from the dice game and half his brain on the ground. A.T. heard the sound of the gun and knew what just happened.

**

Pillz rode through Amityville and pulled over when he saw Muncha posted on the block talking to a few niggas. He rolled down his window and looked at him. "Yo, Muncha get in, baby boy."

"Word, look at Mr. Money pulling up in the big body." Muncha smiled as he got into the truck. "I see you big baller, all caked up now."

"Naw, man, I'm just trying to live. You busy?"

"Naw, what's up?"

"Shit, I was just riding around. You want to ride with me?"

"Shit, take off."

Pillz pulled off. "So, how's the money out here?"

"Money still flowing like clockwork. I heard you be in the Dance now."

"I'm wherever the money at."

"You know A-Dog got a lot of this shit on lock now."

"I'm happy for the nigga. Let him get his bread up."

"Yo, Pillz, you know I fuck with you hard, and I fuck with A-Dog hard. Shit wasn't supposed to go that way with you. Everyone was eating when you were together."

"I tried more than one time to kill that beef and I ended up getting shot. Trying to make peace with them niggas got me setup and almost bodied. At the end of the day, they wanted gunplay, so I pulled up for the smoke."

"Damn, low key, I ain't know that shit."

"Man it ain't no pressure. How are you out here? Are you good?"

"I'm living, fam. That's all that matters."

Pillz fucked with Muncha hard. He was a real one from day one. Pillz pulled over in the Flat Tops at Burger King. "Yo, check me out, fam." Pillz pulled out a quarter kilo and handed it to Muncha. "Look, that's a quarter bird, fam. Get on your feet the right way and come see me. There's enough money out here so we can all eat."

"Yo, that's love, fam?"

"Come on, you know you are one of my days ones. I just want to see you eat, fam."

"That's love."

"Look, Muncha, I got to head out. So, here's my math. Hit my line when you ready to see me again."

"Facts." Muncha dapped Pillz up as he stepped out of his truck. Pillz nodded at him and pulled off, playing Jay-Z's Rock Boy.

Chapter Forty-One

"A-Dog that shit the other night was hot. What was you thinking, bodying son out there in front of everybody like that?"

"That nigga set Tuggy up in the worst way. I had to handle that business. T.T., it wasn't no other way."

"Yeah, I feel you but there's other ways to do shit that don't make the block hot, but shit, you been laying shit down, O.G."

"Yeah and I need your help on the other body that I need to lay down, fam."

"Who the victim?"

A-Dog looked at T.T. with a serious face. "That bitch ass Officer Dererick that be riding around here. Word got back to me he's the one who kidnapped Tuggy and had him killed for Pillz pussy ass."

"Yeah, I heard something like that, but I didn't know how true it was."

"Yeah, that shit was a fact. I'll show his ass that badge don't mean shit to me. He can die just like anybody else can."

"You know I was staying out of you and Pillz beef but I'm down for the one-eight-seven on the boys in blue. When you trying to do that?"

"Soon. I been watching his beat. I just need to get the timing right. Then, we are going to roll his ass."

"Say less. Let's eat on his ass, then."

A-Dog gave T.T. a pound as they sat in his car on the block, making their plans.

**

"Mo'nay, where you at, beautiful?"

"I'm in the kitchen."

Pillz walked into the kitchen and saw Mo'nay at the table eating green grapes. Pillz walked up to her and kissed her on the forehead.

"How did it go out there today."

Pillz sat across from Mo'nay. He pulled her bowl of green grapes over to him and ate one.

Excuse me. I got that bowl of grapes for me and the baby, not you."

"I thought we was sharing."

"Well, we are not." Mo'nay reached across the table and took the bowl back.

"I see you was for real."

"I was, and you never answered my question."

"I pulled up on Buckshot and handed him a kilo two days ago. So, today I rode through Amityville and saw Muncha and gave him a quarter key and told him to hit my line when he's ready to see me again."

"How much did you charge him?"

"Nothing."

Mo'nay looked at Pillz funny when he said that. "I don't understand nothing. Is that a new number I don't know about?"

"A-Dog got the blocks on lock. Niggas really ain't eating out there. Muncha been a real one from day one. If he move the way I want him to; he will be calling me back for a half a bird with the money up front. I can have him pushing for me in Amityville and Buckshot in the Dance and I'm out the picture all the way. The only time they need to see my face is when it's time to reup."

"Well, you know that was smart in a way. You bought his loyalty today. I like that, bae. You're thinking now."

"I been thinking. That's why you got that muffin in the oven cooking now."

"Oh, you planned this?"

"No, I just got a weak pullout game."

"Shut up, silly." Mo'nay threw a grape at Pillz as she sat at the table smiling at him.

**

Muncha was posted upon the corner when A.T. walked up to him. "Now this is new. I ain't seen you out here in a while on the block."

"Shit changes sometimes. Plus, I got that pure cocaine rocked up."

"You should have said that from the beginning. I got the Gs. Fuck with me."

"You know I got you."

"Good because A-Dog is only selling weight. He acting like us smokers ain't the ones who got him where he at today. Now, he's too good for twenty and thirty dollars."

"You know how that shit go."

"Sure fucking do. So, where you going to be at when I need more?"

"Right here till six tonight. Then, I'll be in the corner house in the Flat Tops before you go down the hill."

"Okay, well you got my money and I'll let it be known who got the block now."

"You do that and there will be something in there for you too, A.T."

"You young guys say what? Say no more, right?"

"Real talk." Muncha laughed when A.T. said that and walked off holding that rock in her hand.

**

A-Dog sat in the strip club's back corner smoking a Black & Mild, taking shots of Cîroc. He was watching the dancers on the poles move to Lil' Jon and Usher's Yeah. King Rich walked up to him.

"You ain't popping bottles tonight, just shots?"

"King Rich, what's up fam? Yeah, just a few shots, that's all. Damn, what you doing up in here?"

"You see the little thick red bone on the last pole?"

"Yeah, I see baby girl?"

"Her name's Diamond. I been breaking in her walls for the last few weeks. She gets off in about an hour. I just pulled up and saw you up in here, fam."

"Word, I see you still on your pimp shit."

"It's the oldest game in the world and you can't lose with a flock of bad bitches that crack their purses open. I get them dead faces and they get daddy's dick."

"I hear you; I'm stuck on the white rock game."

"This game ain't for everybody, but, on another note I'm sorry to hear about Tuggy. He was a stand up nigga."

"Yeah, thanks man. That was my round."

"I saw that boy Pillz the other day too, riding down Albany Ave."

"What kind of car he had?"

"He was in a big body Lincoln truck. He had that boy Muncha with him."

"That nigga Muncha is playing it like that?

"I ain't knowing what they had going on, but Lady Red just got off stage. Let me go take care of my business, fam."

"Cool, and good looking out on that story line too."

King Rich threw up two fingers as he walked away from A-Dog's table. A-Dog took his last shot of Cîroc, got up and left the strip club.

Chapter Forty-Two

A-Dog rode up on Muncha as he was standing in front of the pink store. He stepped out of his black Range Rover and walked up to Muncha. "Yo Muncha, what's this I'm hearing about you out here riding around with Pillz?"

"Yeah, he pulled up on me and I jumped in the whip. We rode out for a minute and talked. At the end of the day, you and that nigga is beefing. He is still Browns and that overrides everything."

"You sound crazy as fuck. That nigga had Tuggy bodied, that niggas Browns flag got revoked and he got put on the grocery list. That boy is takeout food and anybody who is fucking with him is too."

"Look, A- Dog, you beefing with the wrong niggas. You pulling up on me sideways because of your beef. Look, I'm Browns and until the brick houses says otherwise part my back."

"Yo', nigga. You heard what the fuck I said too."

Muncha ain't pay A-Dog no mind as he walked off down Smith Street with his hand on the inside of his coat, holding his gun just in case A-Dog tried something.

T.T. saw A-Dog and walked up to him. "What was that about, A-Dog?" I was on my way over here when I saw you and Muncha arguing."

"That's a dead nigga. He out here riding around with Pillz knowing he had Tuggy bodied."

"That nigga was just with Pillz?"

"Fucking right."

"Shit, let's pull up on that now."

"Not today. I got the four one one on that bitch ass officer Dererick. I was just about to pull up on you before I saw that lame as nigga."

"What's the verdict on it?"

"Come on, get in the truck and I'll tell you. I don't need this shit getting out." A-Dog looked at Muncha still walking down Smith Street as he got in his truck. He pointed his hand at him like he had a gun.

**

"Every time you pull up you looking like new money baby. If it ain't in the big body truck, you in the big body Benz."

"Come on man, I'm just trying to eat. Nothing more, Buckshot."

"Shit, I'm trying to eat too."

"That's why I'm here. What you got for me?"

"That forty Gs you asked for."

"My nigga. Let's handle the business then."

"Yeah, that shit been pumping through the hood. Motherfuckers still beating down my door."

"I told you I got that butter. I should put that boy Fabio with the long hair and no shirt on the front of these bricks saying, *I can't believe this that butter.*"

"You funny as fuck, man." Buckshot handled Pillz the forty grand in a black bag. "You want a beer?"

"Is it Coors Lite?"

"You know it is already."

"Yeah, then let me get one with the mountains blue."

"You got time for a blunt?"

"Yeah, I'll post up for a minute, fam."

**

'Look, be on point. We can't afford no slip ups. This is Dererick's beat, and he comes in this store every night to get a coffee for him and his partner. I'm already going to be in the store. As soon as you hear the shots, take out his partner. Meet me at the back of the building and we out."

"I'm on point. I'm ready."

"Say less, I'm going inside now." A-Dog walked in the store to the back where the slot machines were and waited for Officer Dererick to walk in. He took out his gun and cocked it back. He looked at the time on his wristwatch. It was six thirty p.m. on the head when he heard the sound of the store door opening.

"Good evening, Officer Dererick."

"Hey, Roger, how goes it tonight?"

"Good, it's quiet."

A-Dog walked up the ally. "Officer."

Dererick looked at A-Dog as he was letting shots off to his chest. He ran up to Dererick and shot him three times in the face. Dererick's partner jumped out of the car and ran to the store door. T.T. ran up behind him, shooting him in the head and dropping him. He opened up the store door and saw A-Dog with his gun to the store clerk's head. "Give me the fucking video tape. Now!" A-Dog got the video tape and shot the store clerk two times in the head, killing him. "Come on, we out."

A-Dog and T.T. both ran out the back door, through the hole in the fence and to the path to the Flat Tops where they had a car waiting on them. Within thirty minutes, Albany Avenue had over forty policemen out stopping cars, patting people down and asking questions.

**

Pillz looked at his phone and saw that Muncha was calling him back to back. He passed the blunt to Buckshot as he answered the phone. "Yo, what's the word?"

"You ain't in the hood, are you?"

Pillz looked at his phone. When he realized what was happening, he got up. "Why what's up?"

"The hood is flooded with them boys right now. I'm talking about fifty plus, stopping cars, searching, and running up in spots."

"What the fuck is going on out there?"

"Two officers got rolled tonight on Albany Ave. at EZ Deli. These motherfuckers ain't playing out here tonight."

"Yo, say less. Let's lay way low for now. I'm headed back to my spot."

"Cool."

Pillz hung up the phone and looked at Buckshot. "Yo, let me get up out of here. Muncha just told me two officers just got killed in Amityville on Albany Ave. and they are about fifty deep right now pulling everything over."

"Hit me when you get to your spot and let me know you made it home."

"Copy that." Pillz dapped Buckshot up, walked to his Benz, got in and drove off.

Chapter Forty-Three

Mo'nay sat on the couch watching the news. The headlines said two officers and a store clerk were shot to death in Amityville, New York last night. Pictures of each victim were displayed on the screen as onsite news cameras showed live video of the EZ Deli storefront where the shooting took place. The Newswoman ended her report saying the police had no suspects at this time.

"I see you're watching the news still."

"Yeah, I am. A-Dog killed them. He knew it was Dererick who got Tuggy for me and if he knew that, that means somebody else does too. We got to find him and kill before the police catch him."

"A-Dog is anything but a rat, Mo'nay."

"Anthony, I don't give a fuck what he is. They will beat that nigga over and over again until they get a confession out of him. We don't need our names coming up in this shit."

"Right now, that nigga is ducked off as deep in the cut as he can get."

"So, you know what? Find him, kill him, and get rid of the problem. I don't care if you have to put a brick on his head. Matter of fact, put two. We just need this motherfucker dead. He's dumb. Who the fuck kills cops?" Mo'nay got up and in an act of rage stomped off up the stairs.

Pillz just let her go vent, not saying anything to her. He pulled out his phone and called Muncha. He picked up after a few seconds.

"Yo, yo."

"I got two of them things on A-Dog's head and whoever he is with. There's a time limit on this though. Seventy-two hours. I need him peter rolled."

"Say less."

Pillz hung up the phone and walked up the stairs behind Mo'nay.

**

"T.T., it's been six days since we bodied them pigs and they still talking about it on the news. Now, they got a reward out for fifty Gs."

Man, we clear. Don't nobody know shit. We did that shit all the way right."

"We did but A.T. was the one who told me that D-Nice was talking to Dererick. So, if anybody is going to put two and two together, it's going to be her and fifty Gs sounds really good to a basehead."

"So what, you want to kill the bitch?"

"We don't have a choice in the matter. We have to kill her."

"So, when you trying to do this?"

"I can't. I need you to handle this business. I don't need her to see it coming. Once she's out of the way, we can go back to making this money. Plus, I have to drop something off to a few people before they come knocking at my door. I'm already a few days behind."

"Shit, I'll get on that tonight then. I know where she be at." A-Dog nodded his head as he continued to watch the news report on the cop killing in Amityville.

**

Muncha walked down Smith Street to Albany Avenue. He tried to stay as close to the side of the street as possible. The block was still hot and he ain't want to get caught slipping with a gun on him. He walked behind the red house on the corner of Smith Street to cross Albany Avenue without being seen. He heard someone call his name from inside an abandoned house.

"Muncha, Muncha." He turned around and saw it was A.T.

"A.T., I swear you be everywhere in the cut."

"Shit, that's how you have to move out here. The police is every-fucking-where. You know who got the whole damn block on fire doing that crazy shit?"

"Wait, you know who did that shit?"

A.T. looked around with eyes as big and glassy as half dollars from the last hit of dope she took. "Shit, A-Dog killed them cops."

"Why the fuck would he do that?"

"Because they was the ones who got Tuggy and set him up to be killed. I heard that's why A-Dog killed D-Nice, because he setup right over there at Friendly Barbershop."

"Now this shit is starting to make sense. A.T., who else knows about this?"

"I'm guessing just me and you. I saw him a few days ago with that boy T.T. bad ass."

"A.T stay ducked off; the streets is hot right now." Muncha reached into his pocket and pulled out a sack of dope and gave A.T two grams. She smiled wide, showing a row of broken yellow teeth as she took the dope from Muncha. "A.T, I mean it. Stay out of these streets. It's not good for you to be out here right now."

"I'm about to go back in this house and you ain't going to see me no more."

Muncha watched as A.T went back into the crack house. He knew now why Pillz put two kilos on A-Dog's head and whoever he was with. He ain't want his secret to get out in the streets.

**

T.T sat in a black Toyota across the street in the yard from a Baptist church with his gun on his lap, watching the block. He saw a few police drive by, going towards Great Neck Road. He stepped out of the car and walked behind the church to the path leading to the red house. He ain't see nobody, so he walked up Smith Street to the cut that went to the Junior High School. He still ain't see nobody out and posted up behind a tree in the cut so nobody could see him as he watched the block, looking for A.T.

**

"A-Dog, you're a week late. I thought you forgot about me."

"No, it's been so much going on with the beef between me and Mo'nay and cop killing shootouts. My plate's just been full."

"Everybody's plate is full, but here's the thing, when Big Country expects his payment, I can't tell him A-Dog have a lot on his plate right now. Everybody answers to somebody, and everybody has a boss. In Florida, we got Big Country and in Long Island you got me. Five hundred thousand was the original price. Now, I'm adding another fifty grand as a late fee. Payment is up front from here on out. You dropped the egg but it ain't crack because I'm still dealing with you. The point is you dropped the egg. Let this be a life lesson learned for the future, A-Dog."

"I respect that, Manny."

Manny nodded at A-Dog as he left the shop.

"Manny, why didn't you just give him the kilos. You know if he's beefing with Mo'nay, he just can't move reckless."

"Jake, I like A-Dog, really I do. He's hungry but Mo'nay will have him killed before all this is over and I will not lose one kilo over his mistake when he gets a bullet in his head."

**

T.T was standing by a tree smoking when he saw A.T coming from the path by EZ Deli. A red car picked her up in front of the store and drove off, heading towards the Flat Tops. He knew she was headed to buy dope and nine out of ten times, she was going to get dropped off and walk back through the path. He flicked his smoke and went to the path to wait for A.T to walk back. One thing was for sure about a smoker. If they have information, they can sell to get high. It was as good as sold. Their loyalty was to the rock and nothing else. T.T. heard the sound of someone walking through the path. He stood behind the tree and looked at A.T. T.T. pulled his gun out and held it by his side. As A.T. walked by, he closed his eyes and held his breath as he jumped on her. All you heard was the shots of his gun going off and A.T's body hitting the ground. T.T shot her two more times in the head before making his way down the path to the Flat Tops.

Chapter Forty-Four

"How that go with A.T?" A-Dog looked at T.T. as he was drinking a forty ounce of beer and smoking a blunt. "That shit is taken care of. She's dead in the path. What Manny talking about?"

"Nothing that I wanted to hear. He taxed niggas fifty Gs for a late fee. Plus, he went brand new on us and wants all bread up front now."

"What the fuck?"

"Yeah, but don't trip. We going to get right again, hands down. The big picture is we got A.T. out the way and that's all that counts."

"Now, we just got to get this nigga and we back on the money train."

"No, Mo'nay need to be bodied. Then, we can watch Pillz fall apart before we body his ass."

"You know I'm with whatever. I'm down for the ride."

"That's why I put my trust in you, baby boy."

A-Dog patted T.T. on the back. "Come on, let's ride out."

"Copy that."

**

"That shit was fucked up. Yeah, she ran her mouth off too much but A.T. ain't fuck with nobody, B-God."

"Everyone knows that Muncha. I know LaLa was fucked up when she saw her laid out in the path face down in blood and mud."

Muncha and B-God stood under the storefront shed talking as it was raining. Muncha saw the big body Benz pull up and stop a few feet from the store. "Yo, B-God stay up. Let me go take care of this business real quick."

"You know where to find me at, fam."

"Already."

Muncha walked off and got into the Benz. B-God watched as it pulled off.

"How we looking out here, Muncha?"

"The money is flowing. Shit was just starting to pick back up again until the fuck shit happened last night and early this morning."

Pillz looked at Muncha when he said that. "What fuck shit happened? What you talking about?"

"Lala found A.T.'s body in the path last night. She was shot six times. What's so crazy is I was just talking with her last night and I told her to stay out the streets."

"Damn, I fucked with A.T. Do they know who did it?"

"Hell no. Nobody seen shit."

"Somebody knows something. They just ain't talking. What's good with that other conversation we had a few days ago?"

"That boy been M.I.A. Ain't nobody seen him. You know how A-Dog move already. He's waiting for you to slip up or relax so he can put a hole in your head."

"You can't catch a nigga slipping who never sleeps."

"Big facts."

"How much you holding right now?"

"Not even an ounce from the shit you gave me."

"So, you ready to reup then?"

"Yeah, I was really waiting to knock off the last little bit but fuck it, let's do it."

"How much you playing with?"

"Twelve Gs."

"I'll give you a half a kilo and you owe me nine Gs. You can rock with that?"

"Hell yeah. Take me by my spot so I can get the B-love for you."

"You still over the Bridge on Madison Ave.?"

"Yeah."

Pillz nodded and turned the radio up, blasting Meek Mill.

**

Mo'nay pulled up at the park and saw Buckshot talking to a few people. She pulled out her best bad bitch shades, stepped out of her white G-Wagon and started walking towards them.

"Yo, Shots, who the fuck is that bad bitch walking this way?"

Buckshot turned around and saw Mo'nay walking his way. "Oh shit, that's Dope Boy's wife. Y'all niggas hold up. I'll be back in a minute." Buckshot walked up to Mo'nay. "What's up, Mo'nay? It's crazy to see you down here."

"I used to be in this park all the time, Buckshot. I'm not one of them innocent green bitches that just cute and stay at home."

"I already know. Dope Boy got him a real one. So, what's up? What brings you around here?"

Mo'nay looked at Buckshot seriously. "I'm looking for a predator. Someone hungry enough to kill when asked to and who is willing to take the risk for the reward."

"This is about that shit with A-Dog and Pillz?"

"He talked to you about this already?"

"Yeah, a few weeks ago."

"So, why is he still alive then?"

"He told me he had a few guys in the Ville that was going to take care of it."

"You know why I named Anthony Dope Boy?"

"I didn't even know you gave him that name."

"Yeah, I did because Anthony is the definition of a real hustler. He can sell fire in hell and an angel to God. He will kill if he has to but he's not a killer. He's already broke rule number one of being a killer: Never get shooters in your backyard to kill in your backyard. That's the whole point of out of town shooters who come to town and leave when the job is done."

"So, that's why you're here today? Looking for an out of town shooter?"

"No, I think I found one already. Did I, Buckshot?"

"Yeah, where can I find him at?"

"On Smith Street. I trust this conversation will stay between the two of us."

Buckshot looked at Mo'nay and nodded.

"Good, because there's two kinds of respect and two different payments for each one. You will see my payment is different from Pillz, as you call him. Mo'nay looked at Buckshot, opened her Gucci bag, and pulled out two Glock forties and handed them to him. "Both are clean and fully loaded. Hopefully, I will be hearing something on the news tonight."

Buckshot took both guns and placed them in the waist line of his pants. Mo'nay went in her Gucci bag again and pulled out an envelope and handed it to Buckshot. "Like I said, me and Anthony's payments are different. There is forty grand in there."

Buckshot just looked at Mo'nay. "I'll take acre of this tonight."

"Good." Mo'nay got up and walked away, not looking back.

Buckshot knew why Pillz acted and moved the way he did, because he had a boss bitch who made him.

Chapter Forty-Five

"A-Dog we can't be moving like this. The block is hot and the police are still looking for cop killers and the two people that's responsible for the bodies that was in that house fire. We need to find one spot, post up and try to get back to the money."

"We good. T.T. Niggas get killed every day and they know that shit. I don't' want to be posted up in a house and get caught down bad. You feel me."

"Yeah, I feel you."

A-Dog pulled over on the side of the street and looked at T.T. "Motherfuckers know who I am in these streets, and they know my gun game is for real. Now, you rocking with me? We going to take this shit by storm. Trust me, bro."

"I already know."

Muncha was on the corner looking at A-Dog's Range Rover. He pulled his gun out and looked around. A-Dog was rolling up a blunt as him and T.T. listened to NBA YoungBoy. Muncha ran up on the passenger side of the Range Rover dressed in all black. When T.T looked to the side, it was too late. Bullets started flying through A-Dog's window. T.T. was shot two times in the head, killing him on the spot. A-Dog put the car in gear and took off with blood all over his face and windshield. A-Dog was looking at T.T.'s dead body. He started to look back in his rearview mirror. He ain't notice he was shot in his right arm. A-Dog looked at T.T. again, laying there dead. He lost feeling in his arm and crashed into a parked car. He hit his head on the steering wheel. A black SUV pulled up in front of them and two guys jumped out with AR-15's and started shooting up A-Dog's truck. A-Dog was slumped over trying not to get hit as they was shooting up the truck. One of the guys walked up to the door and opened it up. A-Dog looked at him with blood all over him and sweat pouring down his face. The guy nodded at A-Dog and A-Dog just watched as the sparks came out of the AR-15 and felt his body being ripped apart as the bullets went through him. The masked man grabbed A-Dog's dead body and pulled it out the truck, dropped it on the ground and shot him a few more times before jumping in the SUV and pulling off. People stood shocked as they stared at A-Dog's bullet torn body and replayed the violent scent that just took place before their eyes.

**

Pillz looked at his phone as it was going off. He saw it was Muncha calling him. "Yeah?"

"We need to talk."

"About what?"

"That B.I. got taken care of but someone else joined the party."

Pillz walked outside on the back deck of the house. "What you mean someone else joined the party."

"Just like I said. I did my part and a black van pulled up and went O.D. on them both. I'm talking about overkill. Two hundred rounds. His body painted to the ground."

"Where you at?'

"Bayview."

"Meet me at the park in twenty minutes."

"I'm on my way now."

Pillz hung up the phone and walked back into the house.

"Mo'nay, I got to go check on something. I'll be back in a few."

Mo'nay walked to the room door and looked at Pillz as he was walking out the door. She walked back to her bedroom and picked up her phone and was looking at the pictures that Buckshot sent her of A-Dog's dead body outside of his truck. She replied back to his message with a thumbs up and laid her phone down.

**

Pillz stepped out of his Benz and walked up to Muncha as he was smoking a Newport in the park. "Yo, now what you mean someone else joined the party?"

"I been laying on them niggas all day. I saw when he pulled up on the block. Niggas was rolling up in the truck. I ran up on the side and let off. I head checked T.T. A-Dog hit the gas and I let off a few shots and knocked the back window out. They made it to the end of the road, but I guess I hit A-Dog because he crashed the Range Rover into a parked car. Then, out of nowhere these assassins pull up, jump out with AR-15's and go bananas. I'm talking about I saw them drag A-Dog out the car and just stand over him and let loose. It was ugly. They jumped back in the SUV and took off.

Pillz just looked at Muncha as he was talking. "And you don't know who it was?"

"Fuck no. I just know whoever sent them wanted the job done right and they took it to heart."

"You think they knew what truck they was looking for already or did they follow you to get to him?"

"I think they knew exactly who they were looking for. There was no walking away from that. Even if a nigga had on the whole armor of God."

"You know what? At the end of the day, the job is done and them niggas is rolled. I got some other shit I need to check out, so I'll pull back up on you later."

"Copy that."

Pillz dapped Muncha up then walked back to his Benz. Something wasn't right and he needed to know who was in that SUV.

Chapter Forty-Six

"Man, Buckshot, that shit was like a movie how niggas pulled up and just sprayed that nigga shit down. Then, how you just opened the door, pulled him out and went O.D. on them niggas. We made a point out there in the Ville."

Buckshot nodded at his right hand man, Ice-Burg as he was talking. "Yeah, we did that, hands down. We pulled up like we was on some Training Day shit with no talking. But look, this stays between us. Mo'nay don't want nobody knowing about this shit, not even Pillz, homie."

"Say less, bro. I already know. We don't need this shit coming back on us at all."

"That's a fact, fam."

"So, what's the move now?"

"We play the block and get this money up. Pillz dropped two birds off on us and we need to get this bread up now."

"Shit, let's go make it happen then, fam."

**

Pillz walked into the house and up to the table where Mo'nay was sitting. He bent over and gave her a kiss on the forehead and sat down next to her. "Is everything okay, Anthony?"

"Yeah, everything is good. We won't be dealing with A-Dog no more. He's dead as of last night."

Mo'nay looked at Pillz when he said that. "Good, now you can get someone to take over Amityville that you trust."

"Yeah, I can."

Mo'nay grabbed Pillz's hand and pulled him up for a kiss as she looked into his eyes. Mo'nay made Pillz into what she needed him to be, and some conversations didn't need to be talked about. She did what she had to do, and she crushed her enemies totally. She made sure there wasn't even a spark to start up a fire. Not saying that Pillz couldn't do it, but everyone knows that behind every strong man is a stronger woman that speaks quietly in his ear to open his eyes.

To Be Continued…
Gorillaz in the Trenches 3
Coming Soon

Lock Down Publications and Ca$h Presents assisted publishing packages.

BASIC PACKAGE $499

Editing

Cover Design

Formatting

UPGRADED PACKAGE $800

Typing

Editing

Cover Design

Formatting

ADVANCE PACKAGE $1,200

Typing

Editing

Cover Design

Formatting

Copyright registration

Proofreading

Upload book to Amazon

LDP SUPREME PACKAGE $1,500

Typing

Editing

Cover Design

Formatting

Copyright registration

Proofreading

Set up Amazon account

Upload book to Amazon

Advertise on LDP Amazon and Facebook page

***Other services available upon request. Additional charges may apply

Lock Down Publications

P.O. Box 944

Stockbridge, GA 30281-9998

Phone # 470 303-9761

Submission Guideline

Submit the first three chapters of your completed manuscript to ldpsubmissions@gmail.com, subject line: Your book's title. The manuscript must be in a .doc file and sent as an attachment. Document should be in Times New Roman, double spaced and in size 12 font. Also, provide your synopsis and full contact information. If sending multiple submissions, they must each be in a separate email.

Have a story but no way to send it electronically? You can still submit to LDP/Ca$h Presents. Send in the first three chapters, written or typed, of your completed manuscript to:

LDP: Submissions Dept
Po Box 944
Stockbridge, Ga 30281

DO NOT send original manuscript. Must be a duplicate.

Provide your synopsis and a cover letter containing your full contact information.

Thanks for considering LDP and Ca$h Presents.

NEW RELEASES

SKI MASK MONEY 2 by RENTA

BORN IN THE GRAVE 3 by SELF MADE TAY

PROTÉGÉ OF A LEGEND 3 by COREY ROBINSON

GORILLAZ IN THE TRENCHES 2 by SAYNOMORE

SAYNOMORE

STRAIGHT BEAST MODE III

De'Kari

KINGPIN KILLAZ IV

STREET KINGS III

PAID IN BLOOD III

CARTEL KILLAZ IV

DOPE GODS III

Hood Rich

SINS OF A HUSTLA II

ASAD

YAYO V

Bred In The Game 2

S. Allen

THE STREETS WILL TALK II

By Yolanda Moore

SON OF A DOPE FIEND III

HEAVEN GOT A GHETTO III

SKI MASK MONEY III

By Renta

LOYALTY AIN'T PROMISED III

By Keith Williams

I'M NOTHING WITHOUT HIS LOVE II

SINS OF A THUG II

TO THE THUG I LOVED BEFORE II

IN A HUSTLER I TRUST II

By Monet Dragun

QUIET MONEY IV

EXTENDED CLIP III

THUG LIFE IV

By **Trai'Quan**

THE STREETS MADE ME IV

By **Larry D. Wright**

IF YOU CROSS ME ONCE III

ANGEL V

By **Anthony Fields**

THE STREETS WILL NEVER CLOSE IV

By K'ajji

HARD AND RUTHLESS III

KILLA KOUNTY IV

By Khufu

MONEY GAME III

By Smoove Dolla

JACK BOYS VS DOPE BOYS IV

A GANGSTA'S QUR'AN V

COKE GIRLZ II

COKE BOYS II

LIFE OF A SAVAGE V

CHI'RAQ GANGSTAS V

SOSA GANG III

BRONX SAVAGES II

BODYMORE KINGPINS II

By Romell Tukes

MURDA WAS THE CASE III

Elijah R. Freeman

AN UNFORESEEN LOVE IV

BABY, I'M WINTERTIME COLD III

By **Meesha**

QUEEN OF THE ZOO III

By **Black Migo**

SAYNOMORE

CONFESSIONS OF A JACKBOY III

By Nicholas Lock

KING KILLA II

By Vincent "Vitto" Holloway

BETRAYAL OF A THUG III

By Fre$h

THE MURDER QUEENS III

By Michael Gallon

THE BIRTH OF A GANGSTER III

By Delmont Player

TREAL LOVE II

By Le'Monica Jackson

FOR THE LOVE OF BLOOD III

By Jamel Mitchell

RAN OFF ON DA PLUG II

By Paper Boi Rari

HOOD CONSIGLIERE III

By Keese

PRETTY GIRLS DO NASTY THINGS II

By Nicole Goosby

LOVE IN THE TRENCHES II

By Corey Robinson

IT'S JUST ME AND YOU II

By Ah'Million

FOREVER GANGSTA III

By Adrian Dulan

GORILLAZ IN THE TRENCHES III

By SayNoMore

THE COCAINE PRINCESS VIII

By King Rio

CRIME BOSS II

Playa Ray

LOYALTY IS EVERYTHING III

Molotti

HERE TODAY GONE TOMORROW II

By Fly Rock

REAL G'S MOVE IN SILENCE II

By Von Diesel

GRIMEY WAYS IV

By Ray Vinci

Available Now

RESTRAINING ORDER **I & II**

By **CA$H & Coffee**

LOVE KNOWS NO BOUNDARIES **I II & III**

By **Coffee**

RAISED AS A GOON I, II, III & IV

BRED BY THE SLUMS I, II, III

BLAST FOR ME I & II

ROTTEN TO THE CORE I II III

A BRONX TALE I, II, III

DUFFLE BAG CARTEL I II III IV V VI

HEARTLESS GOON I II III IV V

A SAVAGE DOPEBOY I II

DRUG LORDS I II III

SAYNOMORE

CUTTHROAT MAFIA I II
KING OF THE TRENCHES
By **Ghost**
LAY IT DOWN **I & II**
LAST OF A DYING BREED I II
BLOOD STAINS OF A SHOTTA I & II III
By **Jamaica**
LOYAL TO THE GAME I II III
LIFE OF SIN I, II III
By **TJ & Jelissa**
BLOODY COMMAS I & II
SKI MASK CARTEL I II & III
KING OF NEW YORK I II,III IV V
RISE TO POWER I II III
COKE KINGS I II III IV V
BORN HEARTLESS I II III IV
KING OF THE TRAP I II
By **T.J. Edwards**
IF LOVING HIM IS WRONG…I & II
LOVE ME EVEN WHEN IT HURTS I II III
By **Jelissa**
WHEN THE STREETS CLAP BACK I & II III
THE HEART OF A SAVAGE I II III IV
MONEY MAFIA I II
LOYAL TO THE SOIL I II III
By **Jibril Williams**
A DISTINGUISHED THUG STOLE MY HEART I II & III
LOVE SHOULDN'T HURT I II III IV
RENEGADE BOYS I II III IV
PAID IN KARMA I II III

SAVAGE STORMS I II III

AN UNFORESEEN LOVE I II III

BABY, I'M WINTERTIME COLD I II

By **Meesha**

A GANGSTER'S CODE I &, II III

A GANGSTER'S SYN I II III

THE SAVAGE LIFE I II III

CHAINED TO THE STREETS I II III

BLOOD ON THE MONEY I II III

A GANGSTA'S PAIN I II III

By J-Blunt

PUSH IT TO THE LIMIT

By **Bre' Hayes**

BLOOD OF A BOSS **I, II, III, IV, V**

SHADOWS OF THE GAME

TRAP BASTARD

By **Askari**

THE STREETS BLEED MURDER **I, II & III**

THE HEART OF A GANGSTA I II& III

By **Jerry Jackson**

CUM FOR ME I II III IV V VI VII VIII

An **LDP Erotica Collaboration**

BRIDE OF A HUSTLA **I II & II**

THE FETTI GIRLS **I, II& III**

CORRUPTED BY A GANGSTA I, II III, IV

BLINDED BY HIS LOVE

THE PRICE YOU PAY FOR LOVE I, II ,III

DOPE GIRL MAGIC I II III

By **Destiny Skai**

WHEN A GOOD GIRL GOES BAD

SAYNOMORE

By **Adrienne**
THE COST OF LOYALTY I II III
By Kweli
A GANGSTER'S REVENGE **I II III & IV**
THE BOSS MAN'S DAUGHTERS I II III IV V
A SAVAGE LOVE **I & II**
BAE BELONGS TO ME I II
A HUSTLER'S DECEIT I, II, III
WHAT BAD BITCHES DO I, II, III
SOUL OF A MONSTER I II III
KILL ZONE
A DOPE BOY'S QUEEN I II III
TIL DEATH
By **Aryanna**
A KINGPIN'S AMBITON
A KINGPIN'S AMBITION **II**
I MURDER FOR THE DOUGH
By **Ambitious**
TRUE SAVAGE I II III IV V VI VII
DOPE BOY MAGIC I, II, III
MIDNIGHT CARTEL I II III
CITY OF KINGZ I II
NIGHTMARE ON SILENT AVE
THE PLUG OF LIL MEXICO II
CLASSIC CITY
By **Chris Green**
A DOPEBOY'S PRAYER
By **Eddie "Wolf" Lee**
THE KING CARTEL **I, II & III**
By **Frank Gresham**

THESE NIGGAS AIN'T LOYAL **I, II & III**

By **Nikki Tee**

GANGSTA SHYT **I II &III**

By **CATO**

THE ULTIMATE BETRAYAL

By **Phoenix**

BOSS'N UP **I , II & III**

By **Royal Nicole**

I LOVE YOU TO DEATH

By **Destiny J**

I RIDE FOR MY HITTA

I STILL RIDE FOR MY HITTA

By **Misty Holt**

LOVE & CHASIN' PAPER

By **Qay Crockett**

TO DIE IN VAIN

SINS OF A HUSTLA

By **ASAD**

BROOKLYN HUSTLAZ

By **Boogsy Morina**

BROOKLYN ON LOCK I & II

By **Sonovia**

GANGSTA CITY

By **Teddy Duke**

A DRUG KING AND HIS DIAMOND I & II III

A DOPEMAN'S RICHES

HER MAN, MINE'S TOO I, II

CASH MONEY HO'S

THE WIFEY I USED TO BE I II

PRETTY GIRLS DO NASTY THINGS

By Nicole Goosby

TRAPHOUSE KING **I II & III**

KINGPIN KILLAZ I II III

STREET KINGS I II

PAID IN BLOOD **I II**

CARTEL KILLAZ I II III

DOPE GODS I II

By **Hood Rich**

LIPSTICK KILLAH **I, II, III**

CRIME OF PASSION I II & III

FRIEND OR FOE I II III

By **Mimi**

STEADY MOBBN' **I, II, III**

THE STREETS STAINED MY SOUL I II III

By **Marcellus Allen**

WHO SHOT YA **I, II, III**

SON OF A DOPE FIEND I II

HEAVEN GOT A GHETTO I II

SKI MASK MONEY I II

Renta

GORILLAZ IN THE BAY **I II III IV**

TEARS OF A GANGSTA I II

3X KRAZY I II

STRAIGHT BEAST MODE I II

DE'KARI

TRIGGADALE I II III

MURDAROBER WAS THE CASE I II

Elijah R. Freeman

GOD BLESS THE TRAPPERS I, II, III

THESE SCANDALOUS STREETS I, II, III

FEAR MY GANGSTA I, II, III IV, V

THESE STREETS DON'T LOVE NOBODY I, II

BURY ME A G I, II, III, IV, V

A GANGSTA'S EMPIRE I, II, III, IV

THE DOPEMAN'S BODYGAURD I II

THE REALEST KILLAZ I II III

THE LAST OF THE OGS I II III

Tranay Adams

THE STREETS ARE CALLING

Duquie Wilson

MARRIED TO A BOSS I II III

By Destiny Skai & Chris Green

KINGZ OF THE GAME I II III IV V VI VII

CRIME BOSS

Playa Ray

SLAUGHTER GANG I II III

RUTHLESS HEART I II III

By Willie Slaughter

FUK SHYT

By Blakk Diamond

DON'T F#CK WITH MY HEART I II

By Linnea

ADDICTED TO THE DRAMA I II III

IN THE ARM OF HIS BOSS II

By Jamila

YAYO I II III IV

A SHOOTER'S AMBITION I II

BRED IN THE GAME

By S. Allen

TRAP GOD I II III

RICH $AVAGE I II III

MONEY IN THE GRAVE I II III

By Martell Troublesome Bolden

FOREVER GANGSTA I II

GLOCKS ON SATIN SHEETS I II

By Adrian Dulan

TOE TAGZ I II III IV

LEVELS TO THIS SHYT I II

IT'S JUST ME AND YOU

By Ah'Million

KINGPIN DREAMS I II III

RAN OFF ON DA PLUG

By Paper Boi Rari

CONFESSIONS OF A GANGSTA I II III IV

CONFESSIONS OF A JACKBOY I II

By Nicholas Lock

I'M NOTHING WITHOUT HIS LOVE

SINS OF A THUG

TO THE THUG I LOVED BEFORE

A GANGSTA SAVED XMAS

IN A HUSTLER I TRUST

By Monet Dragun

CAUGHT UP IN THE LIFE I II III

THE STREETS NEVER LET GO I II III

By Robert Baptiste

NEW TO THE GAME I II III

MONEY, MURDER & MEMORIES I II III

By **Malik D. Rice**

LIFE OF A SAVAGE I II III IV

A GANGSTA'S QUR'AN I II III IV

SAYNOMORE

THE STREETS WILL NEVER CLOSE I II III

By K'ajji

CREAM I II III

THE STREETS WILL TALK

By Yolanda Moore

NIGHTMARES OF A HUSTLA I II III

By King Dream

CONCRETE KILLA I II III

VICIOUS LOYALTY I II III

By Kingpen

HARD AND RUTHLESS I II

MOB TOWN 251

THE BILLIONAIRE BENTLEYS I II III

REAL G'S MOVE IN SILENCE

By Von Diesel

GHOST MOB

Stilloan Robinson

MOB TIES I II III IV V VI

SOUL OF A HUSTLER, HEART OF A KILLER I II

GORILLAZ IN THE TRENCHES I II

By SayNoMore

BODYMORE MURDERLAND I II III

THE BIRTH OF A GANGSTER I II

By Delmont Player

FOR THE LOVE OF A BOSS

By C. D. Blue

MOBBED UP I II III IV

THE BRICK MAN I II III IV V

THE COCAINE PRINCESS I II III IV V VI VII

By King Rio

210

KILLA KOUNTY I II III IV

By Khufu

MONEY GAME I II

By Smoove Dolla

A GANGSTA'S KARMA I II III

By FLAME

KING OF THE TRENCHES I II III

by **GHOST & TRANAY ADAMS**

QUEEN OF THE ZOO I II

By **Black Migo**

GRIMEY WAYS I II III

By Ray Vinci

XMAS WITH AN ATL SHOOTER

By Ca$h & Destiny Skai

KING KILLA

By Vincent "Vitto" Holloway

BETRAYAL OF A THUG I II

By Fre$h

THE MURDER QUEENS I II

By Michael Gallon

TREAL LOVE

By Le'Monica Jackson

FOR THE LOVE OF BLOOD I II

By Jamel Mitchell

HOOD CONSIGLIERE I II

By Keese

PROTÉGÉ OF A LEGEND I II III

LOVE IN THE TRENCHES

By Corey Robinson

BORN IN THE GRAVE I II III

SAYNOMORE

By Self Made Tay
MOAN IN MY MOUTH
By XTASY
TORN BETWEEN A GANGSTER AND A GENTLEMAN
By J-BLUNT & Miss Kim
LOYALTY IS EVERYTHING I II
Molotti
HERE TODAY GONE TOMORROW
By Fly Rock
PILLOW PRINCESS
By S. Hawkins

<u>BOOKS BY LDP'S CEO, CA$H</u>

TRUST IN NO MAN

TRUST IN NO MAN 2

TRUST IN NO MAN 3

BONDED BY BLOOD

SHORTY GOT A THUG

THUGS CRY

THUGS CRY 2

THUGS CRY 3

TRUST NO BITCH

TRUST NO BITCH 2

TRUST NO BITCH 3

TIL MY CASKET DROPS

RESTRAINING ORDER

RESTRAINING ORDER 2

IN LOVE WITH A CONVICT

LIFE OF A HOOD STAR

XMAS WITH AN ATL SHOOTER

SAYNOMORE